T0129295

Death Valley
of Texas

Death Valley
of Texas

BARBARA HALL

DEATH VALLEY OF TEXAS

Copyright © 2019 Barbara Hall.

All rights reserved. No part of this book may be used or reproduced by any means, graphic, electronic, or mechanical, including photocopying, recording, taping or by any information storage retrieval system without the written permission of the author except in the case of brief quotations embodied in critical articles and reviews.

This is a work of fiction. All of the characters, names, incidents, organizations, and dialogue in this novel are either the products of the author's imagination or are used fictitiously.

iUniverse books may be ordered through booksellers or by contacting:

iUniverse
1663 Liberty Drive
Bloomington, IN 47403
www.iuniverse.com
1-800-Authors (1-800-288-4677)

Because of the dynamic nature of the Internet, any web addresses or links contained in this book may have changed since publication and may no longer be valid. The views expressed in this work are solely those of the author and do not necessarily reflect the views of the publisher, and the publisher hereby disclaims any responsibility for them.

Any people depicted in stock imagery provided by Getty Images are models, and such images are being used for illustrative purposes only. Certain stock imagery © Getty Images.

ISBN: 978-1-5320-7833-0 (sc)
ISBN: 978-1-5320-7834-7 (e)

Library of Congress Control Number: 2019909817

Print information available on the last page.

iUniverse rev. date: 07/16/2019

CHAPTER 1

It's a beautiful, slightly windy morning here at the open-air market located across the border from Reynosa, Mexico, in a small city called Hidalgo. Hidalgo, Texas, has a population of 13,931 people and is a ten-mile drive to south McAllen. McAllen, Texas, is the largest city in Hidalgo County and the twenty-second-most-populous city in the state; it is located on the southern tip of the state, known as the Rio Grande Valley. Palm trees were likely brought to the valley around the same time citrus was introduced to the region. We now enjoy the palm trees that pepper the South Texas skyline. McAllen is nicknamed the City of Palms.

This area now offers three of the finest medical facilities located in the South Texas region. Most of the hospitals are affiliated with larger hospitals across the country, making them leaders on the cutting edge of the newest medical technology available to date so our residents don't have to travel far to get the best medical care possible. McAllen is the fifth-most-populous developing metropolitan area in

Texas; with the surrounding cities, the population is in excess of 750,000 residents and growing. It has quite the European feel, with all the international museums, Picasso lithographs, and European paintings, as well as bistros, shopping, and now the best medical care available in our area. The languages, diversity of cultures, and different incomes have proven that all sorts of people make this area a great melting pot, and people are drawn from all over the United States and Mexico to utilize what we have available.

This area is a very pleasant and hospitable place. The temperatures are always mild, with a little cold in the winter months. It's nothing like our winter partners who flee from the northern states so they can enjoy the warmth and calm weather we offer in South Texas. We refer to them as snowbirds, and most are retired, but there is an abundance of life and spending from our winter Texans who come from the upper states, who live here for three to six months out of the year. Most own homes in both places and love this area because it is like traveling to Europe without having to use a passport or leave Texas. Our snowbirds fly in, and then when the weather warms, they migrate back to their homes in the upper United States. With the North American Free Trade Agreement, this area has experienced an increase in cross-border trading with Mexico, meaning more people are crossing the border daily. For work or pleasure, traffic has been increasing steadily.

With the first early-morning rays, which were warm and bright, the sun had just risen. The early-morning dew was still on the ground. The open-air market was set up and ready to see its first customers.

"It should be a good day today." Joseph was always optimistic about the sales and how good people would do at the market.

"Yes, it should be," Anna replied.

"Are you ready?"

"Yes, I am open. Thank you for always helping me, Joseph."

"Anytime. See you later."

The market had just opened, and this was where the people gathered to get the freshest of all goods. Meats, cheeses, fruits, and vegetables, along with beautiful tropical plants and flowers that grew in the area, were just a few of the things available for sale.

She is here again, Joseph Garcia thought as he saw her make the next table at the local market.

Mia said, "The mangos are beautiful in color and smell so ripe," as she picked up the fruit one by one, concentrating hard on it as though waiting for it to ripen more in her hand. Then she examined it and smelled it again to make sure it was the one she wanted. With her pouty lips straight out of a dirty dream, she kissed the fruit, lowered it back to the table, and asked Joseph to pack it up. This seemed to be a daily ritual for her.

"How much do I owe you?" Mia asked.

"That will be twenty dollars total."

"Gracias, Joseph."

"De nada, Mia."

Joseph knew the goods she wanted, and it was always one of the biggest sales of the day. He made sure the best fruits and vegetables were available and front and center for Mia to choose from. Mia brought grace and elegance to the market when she shopped. She was about five foot nine inches in height with a body of a ballerina, long and slender with a small bump in her midsection. People loved her and always looked forward to her coming by their booths.

For several months in a row, she came to the market and had the same routine. Everyone was prepared for when she walked by.

Looking at her side profile, one could tell she exuded a natural beauty, not needing much makeup. Every hair was in place as though she got out of bed looking flawless, with little effort to maintain it. She was well dressed and manicured as though she was going to church. Her jewelry was expensive but tastefully done—not the overkill one saw from a lot of Mexican nationals who seemed to think the more jewelry, the better.

The open-air tent partially shaded her beautiful face, but one could tell she took very good care of herself. One of the workers approached her and asked, "¿Estás listo para tener ese bebé todavía?"

"No, not yet, but very soon."

"Motherhood agrees with you. You are glowing."

"Gracias. You are very kind."

Mia lived in Mexico but would cross the border daily to do her shopping. It was typical of people who lived in and around the area and crossed frequently. Most were wealthy, but the area saw all types. It hosted to every walk of life and accommodated everyone. Most people from Mexico loved the South Texas area, and armed with the laser visa in hand, Mexican nationals could come and go as they pleased. Some had homes on this side of the border as well as in Mexico. Typically they came back and stayed here for weeks at a time.

Most of what we offered was more available, and the quality was much better and more convenient than what was offered in Mexico. They found foods like fruits and vegetables, clothing, and much more. The produce was as fresh as could be because they had just been harvested from the fields, and the meats were fresh straight from the farms.

She remarked about how grueling the heat was and how the snowbirds had to get used to the temperatures if they were to continue to travel down this far south and stay. Then she commented she could never live where it was cold because she would not be able to handle the temperatures; she had been born and raised in Mexico and could not survive without the warmth and all the fresh foods and goods she had grown to love so much.

She hadn't been there long when Joseph noticed her. Mia was tall, and one could hardly tell she was pregnant because of how slenderly she carried her baby. She had long black hair and tanned olive-colored Latin skin. He commented on how truly beautiful she was, and today she was just radiant.

Mia blushed and replied, "Gracias, Joseph. You are so kind."

The moment Mia walked around the corner, one could see her beauty from a distance. She would speak to everyone and always asked how they were doing. People thought she was a good person inside and out. People would stop and watch her as she made her way through the market. She always commanded attention from the people around her, whether she wanted it or not. People would gather, stop, talk, and look at her.

"Ms. Mia, we look forward to seeing you tomorrow. Is there anything you need that we can get for you that we didn't have today?"

Mia responded, "I am good, Joseph. I look forward to seeing you tomorrow."

Mia was a caring person, making it a point to acknowledge and respect the people of the area. She felt she would treat people the way she wanted to be treated herself. Mia had a small family she always bought food for so they would be able to eat. There was one little girl in particular whom Mia was fond of, and she looked for her every time she came to the market.

The child was of great beauty and as sweet as could be. She was very polite and well mannered, and she always dressed in traditional Mexican clothing, a shirt and skirt with all the colorful embroideries. She would pull her hair up in a tight bun, and a flower was placed daily to show a true tradition of Mexico. One could tell she was not from a very wealthy family; she always looked as though she needed a bath, and she never wore shoes. Lucy always sought out Mia because she knew if she would dance the traditional dances of Mexico for her, Mia would treat her to food and take care of her with money. Mia always made sure she had enough for Lucy every day.

"Here, Lucy. This is for my last dance before I become a mom."

"Oh, thank you, ma'am."

Mia bent down and told Lucy, "I am not going to be here for a couple of weeks. I want to make sure you have what you need while I am gone."

Lucy was sad, but she knew it was getting close to the time for Mia to have her baby.

Mia said, "Joseph over here is going to give you what you need. I have paid him in advance for you. You just pick what you want, and Joseph will let me know if I need to pay him extra."

"Oh, thank you, Ms. Mia. I can't wait to see the baby."

"Joseph, is our arrangement okay?"

"Yes, ma'am, we are good."

"Joseph, you take care of her till I get back."

"Yes, ma'am, I will."

The farmers market was a great place to shop for freshly baked tortillas, bread, fruits, vegetables, jams, and meats. Mia always made this her last stop in her routine to pick up what she needed before going back across the border. She was eight and half months pregnant and was almost ready for the new addition to be added to her family. Mia knew she would not be able to make many more trips because she was getting so close to her due date, and once the baby was here, she would not want to take the baby out for a while.

Mia had a driver, Juan, who took her daily to shopping, the doctor appointments, hair appointments—whatever she needed. Her last stop before going home was the market. Juan patiently waited outside while she shopped and went to her appointments. He had been hired by her husband to drive her for safety reasons. He always carried her bags back to the car as she completed her shopping routine. He watched her very closely to make sure she was always safe and protected. One could never be too safe crossing the border back and forth in South Texas, and with her husband's job title, sometimes it took an hour or two just to get across the border. It was safer that Juan was there because of the wait time, which could be dangerous. He never let her out of his sight.

"Juan, are you about ready to go back?"

"Whenever you are ready, ma'am. I can do this all day."

She told Juan, "I am feeling a little tired and not too well. I think I overdid it with the extra shopping today, so I think it might be time to finish up. Most days the South Texas heat is unbearable, and today it seemed as though someone turned up the heat."

Juan jumped in the new Mercedes, turned on the car to cool it down for her, and then went around to open the door. "Thank you, Juan. I don't know what I would do without you today. I am feeling extremely tired and am having a few small cramps. I am just worn out. I am ready to head home."

Mia quietly sat in the back seat of the car. She took a deep breath and finally said, "Juan, could you please pull over and buy me a cold bottle of water?"

She explained that she was not feeling well at all. She was starting to feel pressure on her stomach, and it was getting stronger. She wanted to hurry home, get off her feet, and lie down. It was two weeks too early for the baby, and she felt something was wrong. Her head was spinning, and she felt very weak and hot. She thought the water would help if she was overheated from being out too long at the market. South Texas was known for being sweltering at times. She sat back in the seat and blinked her eyes once and then twice. Then everything went black.

Juan had quickly gone inside the store to get the water, but when he returned to the car, Mia was slumped over in the back seat, and he could not get her to respond. "Mia, Mia, wake up! Oh Dios mío, ¿qué voy a hacer necesito ayuda? Please help me!"

He quickly got in the car and got on the phone. "Hello, sir. Something has happened to Mia," he explained. "We were walking through the market just like we always do, and she told me she felt bad and needed to sit down. She was tired and wanted to go, so she got in the car. The next thing I know, she is leaning over in the seat and not responding to anything. Sir, what do you want me to do?"

"Take her to the hospital!"

"Yes, sir. Which one would you like me to take her to? There are three right in a row together."

"Rio Grande Hospital, Juan."

"Sir, I think you need to get here as quick as you can. Mia doesn't look good."

Pablo yelled at Juan, "You'd better not let anything happen to Mia." He hung up on him.

Juan sat for a few seconds before reality kicked in. He sped off to Rio Grande Hospital, located in McAllen, Texas, as quickly as he could. It was a ten-mile drive, and all he kept thinking about was Pablo's last words: "Get her there."

Juan knew what Mia's husband was capable of, and he knew his life was at stake.

Juan drove like a madman. The ten miles between the two towns seemed to go on forever. Weaving in and out and around cars was a hard thing to do in this part of the city, and South McAllen was heavily congested with traffic at this time of day. Juan was honking and driving on the wrong side of the road. People were yelling at him to go back to Mexico if he couldn't drive better than that. He went up and over the curbs, waving his arms at drivers. He started yelling at them to get out of the way and making a few hand gestures. He finally made it to the hospital and pulled into the emergency entrance area.

Juan parked the car, yelled for help, and ran into the entrance. "I need help! I need help getting her out of the car!"

The nursing staff ran to the door to assist him.

Juan said, "She needs to see a doctor as soon as possible. She is not awake or breathing. Hurry, Hurry! I don't want anything to happen to her. Please help her!"

"How far along is she?""

Juan replied, "I really don't know. I think the baby should be here in a couple more weeks."

The emergency room nurse ran with a gurney to the entrance, and they got Mia on it and pushed it into an exam room. "Back up, sir. On three, lift. One, two, three, lift! Okay, she is on. Start CPR," the nurse yelled. "Sir, we can take it from here. Go to the front desk and give them her information. What's your name?"

"Juan," he said. He then explained he did not know a lot of personal information; he was just her driver.

"That's okay. Just give them what you know."

The nurse asked if she had a doctor taking care of her.

Juan replied, "I really have no idea. I drove her to the clinic but can't tell you whom she was seeing." Juan did as he was told, and he went to the desk to provide any information he could because he knew he would be in terrible trouble with the boss if something happened to his wife.

Mia was still unresponsive.

The nurse yelled, "She is pregnant and not responding. The baby's heart rate is in the sixties, and it is not coming up. Call OB. We need to get her up there as soon as we get her stable. Call the OB doctor who is on call."

CHAPTER 2

D
r. Trey Martinez was the doctor on call and was called in to work on Mia. He was a distinguished, board-certified obstetrician/gynecologist who had just been appointed as the department chair. He was a tall, well-dressed, well-mannered, and caring physician. His body was his temple because there was not an ounce of fat on it. His six-pack was well defined and could be seen beneath his tight T-shirt. His hair was groomed, and he had a smile that could cut like a knife. Dr. Martinez took great pride in the way he looked. He loved the way women admired him and his body. He was flattered and appreciated women and the flirting they did, which was a big part of his personality. The nurses would let him know he was the best-looking eye candy this hospital had seen in a long time. If one didn't know he was a doctor, one would think he was a professional model. Dr. Martinez had a mild demeanor, but one shouldn't be fooled because once inside the delivery

room or operating room, he could shout orders like a drill sergeant.

As the department head of ob-gyn for Rio Grande Hospital, he had less time for a personal life. The long-awaited goal of his career and the fight to get here had been a tough one, and as far as he was concerned, it was all well worth it. He was of a Cuban descent and had made his way from Cuba as a small boy to Miami, Florida. After graduating from medical school from the University of Miami with his medical doctor degree, he then continued to earn his PhD. He was very educated, board certified in obstetrics and gynecology, and world renowned in his field. Mia could not have asked for a better physician to care for her.

After living in Miami, Dr. Martinez adjusted to his new life in the Dallas metropolitan area and learned to love Texas as his home. He stayed and practiced in northern Texas until just a few months ago, when Rio Grande Hospital called. The hospital had a reputation for aggressively recruiting high-volume physicians to become investors in their facility, which was partially owned by the doctors in the area, and would have their patients use their facility. Once on staff, they were given carte blanche for anything they needed, and with that in mind, they offered Dr. Martinez a very lucrative contract to relocate and practice medicine in the Valley of Texas. Dr. Martinez and his family looked forward to the change and were excited to relocate to a new city—and for giving them a fresh start to work on their marriage. Dallas was getting a little too big and was hard to get around in with all the traffic and congestion; this made McAllen a great choice. It was a growing city with all the amenities one could ask for, with a bonus of traveling to a foreign country within a couple of miles. This was quite appealing to the doctor and his wife.

Lori was a devoted and loving wife who usually gave in to anything that Dr. Martinez wanted or needed to further his career. This was a stepping stone to help recover their marriage, so she kept telling herself it would all be worth it in the end.

CHAPTER 3

When one pulled up to the main entrance of Rio Grande Hospital, one was met with its valet service for one's car. Then as one entered and come through the automatic doors, it looked just like a fancy hotel, immaculate with marble floors and granite counters. There were fresh flowers everywhere, as well as large statues and Michelangelo prints hanging for decor. This hospital spared no expense on decorating and made guests feel special. It had a new, 503-bed facility with state-of-the-art equipment like PET scans, robotic surgery, and breast imaging, which at one time required trips to Houston and San Antonio. The biggest draw of all was that 750 babies per month were delivered in Rio Grande Hospital, and when born they were American citizens. No one was turned away because of inability to pay, making it one of the most sought-after hospitals in the South. The hospital knew it had excellent medical staff and some of the state's top-notch physicians with impeccable reputations, as well as the best and newest technologies available in the United States, making it a very desirable place.

The people were lucky to have such a great facility here, and this made for great convenience to the people in Texas as well as the people in Mexico who could afford to cross over. It was located in the middle of Hospital Alley in McAllen, Texas; this area had been in great need, and the biggest challenge of all was the number of people seen on a daily basis, with a huge influx of Mexican nationals crossing the border every day seeking medical attention. Most arrived here with no previous medical care or prenatal care of any kind, especially pregnant women. This could prove to be very difficult at times, and Dr. Martinez was about to find out just how much of a challenge it could be.

Most women chose to deliver their babies in McAllen not just because of the new, good-looking OB doctor but because it was the closest medical facility to the border. With the babies born on this side of the border, US citizenship was granted as soon as they enter this world. The parents were free to stay with them with all the amenities of the area. It is a win-win for the Mexican nationals. However, Dr. Martinez was soon to learn that not all births were easy and without serious complications when dealing with the people from Mexico.

CHAPTER 4

D r. Martinez walked in and started ordering all sorts of tests and medications to be administered. He asked for vitals, and then he saw the ultrasound picture of the uterus, which gave him a better understanding of what was happening. He shouted, "We need to move if we are going to try to save this baby's life. Are you coming, Janie? I need as much information from the driver or her family so I can get her medical history."

"What happened?" they asked Juan, but Juan had no idea.

"He kept saying she was fine and complained about being tired. Then she just collapsed."

"Okay, we have a faint pulse. Let's get her upstairs to the operating room. We are going to have to deliver this baby."

"Where is her family?" the nurse asked Juan.

"I am the only one here with her."

"Where is the father of the child?"

"I'm sorry; he is not here yet."

"We need consent to treat."

Juan said, "I have called her husband. He should be here any minute."

The doctor asked, "Who you are?"

"I am her driver. I work for her husband."

At that time, the hospital admittance clerk said, "Excuse me. Can you fill out the paperwork so we can get her treated? What's her name? How old is she? And I need an address. Does she have insurance?"

As Juan was about to answer, he turned and saw her husband had walked through the door.

"Where is Mia? I want to see her right now," Pablo demanded. He told the clerk, "I am Pablo Cruz. I am her husband, and I will be paying cash for everything she and the baby need."

Dr. Martinez stuck his head out and yelled, "Call the OR. We need a C-section. This baby needs to be delivered. Let's go!"

He knew he had good nurses available; they were some of the best in the area. He shouted orders at the crew as they scrambled to get her down the hallway, and they disappeared into the operating room. Janie, a veteran maternity nurse, entered the room.

"Mr. Cruz, we have no time to waste," Dr. Martinez said. "We will be out shortly to speak to you."

Just then, Janie walked up to Dr. Martinez and said, "We don't have consent to treat. I need his consent now so I can start the C-section."

The doctor sent Janie to find Mia's husband.

"Hi, Mr. Cruz. I am Janie. I am a registered nurse working in OB with Dr. Martinez, and he sent me out here to talk to you, get you to sign the consent form, and explain to you about the treatment your wife needs." Janie explained the procedure in detail and let Pablo know his wife was bleeding. She needed a C-section to deliver the baby and stop the bleeding. Janie then told Pablo that without the treatment or procedure for his wife and child, they both could possibly die.

Pablo consented and said to Janie, "Please don't let anything happen to them."

"We are the ones taking care of her. I need you to come with me quickly. I need you to understand and sign the forms that will grant us permission so we may go ahead with the emergency Cesarean section we are going to perform on your wife." She asked several times if he understood how critical the situation was and if he had any questions for her.

Pablo signed the paperwork. "No, I have no questions." He kept asking Janie, "Are Mia and my baby going to be all right?"

"We will be with you as quick as we can," Janie replied. "She is in good hands, and we are doing everything we can."

Pablo's face dropped when he asked Juan, "What happened?"

"I don't know, sir. When she came back to the car, she told me she was tired and ready to go. On the way back to the border, she asked for water. I stopped, got water for her, and returned to the car to find her slumped over."

"Juan you are like family. I told you not to let anything happen to her. Nothing had better happened to her. I will hold you responsible! You go outside and wait for me. Or rather, go home and tell my driver to wait for me."

Juan did as he was told.

Dr. Martinez said, "Get her on the table now!" As soon as they did and the anesthesiologist had her under, the lights were adjusted to the spot where DR. Martinez needed to make the first incision. He cut the first layer, and then the second incision separated the layer of fat. His third cut was a sheetlike layer which was where all the muscles converged. "Here," he said to Janie, handing back the scalpel. "Don't be afraid to move a little faster. This lady is in trouble." The body's underlying tissues were soft and smooth to the touch, and he felt he could rip them faster than he could cut them.

As soon as he had her open, he saw exactly what the problem was and what they were facing. Her placenta had detached. As Dr. Martinez tugged on the umbilical cord and saw the placenta, shiny and purple in color under the lights, it came sliding out with ease. Then he felt a splash against his legs. When he looked down, he saw a large pool of blood on the floor directly under Mia's legs. More blood soaked the gown the doctor wore. He pushed his hands and arms deep inside of Mia to deliver her baby. He also knew how fast she could bleed out if he didn't hurry. A large amount of brownish amniotic fluid poured out of Mia and spread across the operating table. The color told him that the baby was under stress and had his first bowel movement in the sack. If any of this was swallowed by the baby or got in his lungs, it could pose a terrible complication and could lead to death. By now the operating field was drowning in a sea of blood and meconium. It was Dr. Martinez's job to save the life of this mother and baby—and his alone.

"If we stand a chance at saving their lives, we have to move quickly."

Dr. Martinez adjusted himself, working confidently and steady. He pulled carefully yet with determination and conviction to get the baby out. He cut the cord, scooped the baby boy into his arms, and handed him off to Janie. As he did, he noticed the arms and legs hung slack. She rushed him across the operating room to the neonatologist and resuscitation cart that was standing by; nurses were waiting for the viability of the child. The nurses moved out of the way, and no one said a word as the team of people began to work on the baby. The only sounds that came from the room was the beeping of the monitors and the sound of the breathing machine attached to the mother. Dr. Martinez looked at the baby on the cart. Then he looked at the clock to see how much time had passed. The time hit him like a cannon. *This is not good. Too much time has passed.*

"I will start on the mom and get her taken care of." *Good God, this looks like a scene right out of* The Exorcist. *It's a blood bath, and we are losing her!* "Did we cross and type her blood?"

Yes, she is AB positive."

"Okay, hang more blood—she needs it. Open the blood to run it in as fast as it can. Wow, she is bleeding, and I can't seem to stop it." Dr. Martinez decided he needed to do a full hysterectomy if he was going to stop the bleeding. It was Mia only chance at survival.

Just as Dr. Martinez finished up with the final staples, Mia flatlined and went into cardiac arrest. *I was afraid this was going to happen. She lost so much blood; as fast as we put it in, it poured out.* "Call a code blue—stat!"

The code team came running into the room and started working on her. They were a team of providers that rushed to specific locations in the hospital and began immediate resuscitative efforts when a patient was in cardiopulmonary arrest. This hospital had a special team of people to help work on the patient when this happened in the operating room.

They worked on her continuously for an hour before Janie said to Dr. Martinez, "We need to call it. She is still unresponsive and has no pulse."

"Damn it. Okay, calling it. Time of death, 11:00 a.m." *What a way to start the day.* Dr. Martinez was furious because he felt this was such a preventable thing that had happened to this mother and child. With the proper medical care, this would not have gone this far.

Janie patted Dr. Martinez on his back and said, "You did all you could. Come on, Dr. Martinez. Mia was a tough case even for you, she was gone when she got here, and now it's just final. We see stuff like this all the time."

"Janie, don't be so cavalier about this," Dr. Martinez snapped at her. "This is horrible."

Dr. Martinez came out to speak to the family. "Mr. Cruz," he said in Spanish.

Pablo answered the doctor in English. "I understand you."

"Good. I need to speak to you in private, please. Follow me to the consultation room."

"What is going on? Just tell me what has happened to my wife and child."

"Please, Mr. Cruz, have a seat. I am so sorry to tell you this, but your wife and child did not make it. Mia had what we call a placenta previa. If you have this in early pregnancy, it usually is not a problem. However, it can cause serious problems the later it happens in the pregnancy. The placenta would be torn away from its roots during a vaginal delivery, causing life-threatening bleeding for the mom and a lack of oxygen for the baby. Your wife went into labor this morning, and when she was walking around, it caused her to progress more. I don't think she was aware of it until it was too late. This can cause severe bleeding during labor and birth, which put your wife and baby in a fatal situation. Your wife lost so much blood that she went into cardiac arrest, and we couldn't get her heart started again. The baby died from lack of oxygen. Again, I'm so very sorry, Mr. Cruz. If I can do anything for you, please let me know. Let me call the nurse so she can help you make arrangements for your wife and child. "Janie, can you come here and help Mr. Cruz?"

Pablo sat back in the chair, blank-faced. Then he erupted. "How did this happen? She was fine this morning when she left."

Dr. Martinez explained that this could happen very rapidly and without any symptoms until it was too late. "I'm sorry she bled out and went into cardiac arrest. The baby was not responsive upon delivery. We did everything we could possibly do to save them both, but they were too far gone. Your wife lost a lot of blood and could not recover. This is a very hard thing to control. If she had gotten here sooner, there would have been a better chance of saving their lives. I am deeply sorry for your loss."

Janie said, "Mr. Cruz, did you hear me? Can I get you anything or call anyone for you?"

Pablo stood up, blocked the door, and spoke firmly as he lowered his face close to Janie's. "I want nothing from you. Look at my face and hear me. I will do to you and the doctor what you have done to me and my family." He kicked

CHAPTER 5

On Dr. Martinez's way out, he saw Janie in the hallway. Dr. Martinez was shaken but never showed it. He asked, "Janie, are you okay?"

"Yes, Doc. But did you hear what he said to me?"

"Yes, I did. He said it to both of us. I think you need to call security, and they need to make sure Pablo Cruz is gone and out of the hospital before we come out of this area."

Security came and Dr. Martinez explained what had happened.

Janie was totally shaken. Security became concerned and said to Dr. Martinez, "We have had several threats to the doctors and staff here at the hospital, but we have always blown them off. Nothing ever came of them, and because we live on the border of Mexico, they simply think a little differently than we do. We have four of the largest drug cartels that come through the valley of Texas daily, and you really need to be careful."

Dr. Martinez explained, "This lady had no prenatal care and had just shown up in the emergency room. Then I was called in."

"I hear you, Doc, but they won't care about that. They will simply blame the doctor and the people around person who died."

"She was in bad shape when she got here."

The security guard said, "It doesn't matter. They still won't see it that way. They will hold you responsible for her and the baby's lives. You really need to get a security guard to walk you in and out of the hospital and the parking lot."

Doctor Martinez was a little more shaken now. "I have clinic tomorrow. What do I do? Surely no one will enter and do something crazy in there in front of all my patients."

"Don't be too sure of that. All I can say is be careful. It gets a little like the Wild West down here."

"I'm from the Dallas area, and we don't see this kind of stuff up there."

The officer replied, "Anything goes here. Welcome to the Death Valley of Texas."

After a long night, Dr. Martinez finished. He started to go outside before he remembered what the security guard had told him: be diligent. He called to have someone escort him to his car. He said to the guard, "This is nuts. My car is in a secured parking lot. I think I just got a little spooked. I'm good from here."

"You going home, sir?"

"Yes, straight. I am so tired. I have been up for seventy-two hours and am beaten."

As Dr. Martinez made his way to his car, the security guard watched to make sure he got in safe. He waved to let him know he was going back inside. Once in his car, it was so surreal. He quickly locked the doors and turned to make sure no one was in the car with him. Goosebumps popped up all over. Dr. Martinez thought, *My mind is playing tricks on me, and I have always had an overactive imagination.* As he headed out of the parking lot, the electric arm rose up, and he went through the gated area. *I am so glad this night is over.* Exhausted, hungry, and yawning, he looked at the clock on his dash. It was 7:30 a.m., and he had been up all night. He thought, *I had better hurry if I want to eat before the clinic starts.*

While heading home, he decided that because his wife was out of town, he would need to stop to get a quick bite to eat. He had been on call for three days straight and had pretty much been living at the hospital, so he thought a drive-through was well worth the effort. After ordering the food, he headed home but couldn't resist eating his taco as he drove to his house. *I love me some good Mexican tacos.* His wife had him on a strict, healthy diet, so he could eat tacos only when she was not there. He laughed and thought, *If she could only see me now, she would kill me. Which only makes the food taste even better.*

CHAPTER 6

D r. Trey Martinez and his wife owned twenty acres in the middle of town, which gave him great access to all the hospitals. It also allowed him to feel as though he lived in the country but with all the city amenities. It gave him and his wife a very private, peaceful ranch life, but they were located in the middle of the town, to which they had grown accustomed. With all the pastures, horses, and cattle, it was as close to paradise as one could get in South Texas. The gate and property were landscaped and meticulously taken care of. Gorgeous large oak trees lined the driveway as one came up to the main house. There were barns and a small guesthouse located by the pool, and caretakers quarters were located just behind the barn. One could see all the roses and bougainvilleas in bloom, which made the property exquisite in detail. This property had everything anyone could want.

He pulled up to the gate to wait for it to open, and when he drove through, it automatically closed. He noticed no dogs came to greet him. He thought, *That's odd,* but figured they were being lazy; some of them were getting up in age. As he walked up to the back door, he could hear one of the dogs whimpering, but he couldn't figure out what was wrong with him. Neither could he find him. He proceeded to go around the beautifully decorated wrap-around porch, which led to the front of the house. As he followed the cries of the pooch, he made his way around to the front door. He couldn't believe his eyes. "Oh my God! What the hell is this?"

On the door was one of the most horrific scenes, right out of a horror movie. Blood was everywhere, and it looked like his dog, Chicca, had put up a pretty good fight before they ended her life. The worst part was Chicca was disemboweled as she hung from the front door with a knife through her chest, holding her up there.

A horrible note read, "I will do to you as you did to my family!"

All the other dogs were lying there, whimpering; they'd apparently stayed with her through the whole attack. He stumbled back, looking around to see if someone was on the property with him. *Shit! I am a target!* He decided to call for help, reached for his phone, and realized he'd left it in the truck. He ran as quick as he could grabbed it, went in the house, and locked the door, shaking profusely. He finally got his composure and called 911.

Within five minutes, the cops arrived at the gate to the property. "Hello, Dr. Martinez. This is Officer Espinoza with the McAllen Police Department. I was on my way home, and I heard the call. I live a couple of miles down the road."

"Oh, thank you for coming out. I'll open the gate—hang on."

As Officer Espinoza drove down the long, tree-lined driveway, he came up to a beautiful farmhouse that had been renovated and updated. The house looked as though it had come out of a magazine. Dr. Martinez was waiting for him.

"What seems to be the problem?"

Dr. Martinez said, "Please call me Trey, and follow me. I was at work for the past seventy-two hours, and I have not been home until now. I had one hell of a rough night with a patient. We worked on her for hours, but to no avail. She passed away, as did the child. To say the least, the husband was not too happy with me and threatened me."

"Do you know the person's name who threatened you?"

"Yes, he called himself Pablo Cruz."

"Oh crap." Officer Espinoza got on the radio right away and called for backup.

"As I finished my shift I came home to find this." He took Officer Espinoza to the front door.

"Oh Lord. This looks like the signature of one of the largest cartels in the valley. Pablo Cruz is rumored to be the head of it, and he's very ruthless. Dr. Martinez, you made a very dangerous enemy."

CHAPTER 7

"Trey, do you have security on your property? If you don't, you need to get some. It is very important to make sure you have the grounds covered at all times so you are safe. Is there anyone who lives here with you?"

"I am married, but my wife is visiting her daughter out of town right now. She should be home tomorrow."

"Okay, then. Let's secure the property. I'll have some undercover patrolmen to keep you safe for the night until you get permanent security in place, but I have to tell you these people are very ruthless, and they stop at nothing to get what they want. They have eyes everywhere. You will need to be extra careful. When will you be going out again?"

"In about five hours. I have to run the clinic at my office."

"Well, is there any way you can cancel it or cut it back?"

"No, I can't. My wife and I are going on vacation in three weeks, and I need to get all my patients seen before

I go so everyone is covered. I will be there all day and into the evening hours."

"Do you have a lot of staff there?"

"Yes, six to ten of us."

"Okay, you will need to let us check your office to make sure there are no surprises."

Trey rubbed his head. "I can't figure out how they knew where I lived. I just bought the place about a month ago, and my wife and I are new to the area."

"Remember what I said: they have eyes everywhere. If they want to find you, they will. You need to alert your staff and make sure people don't stay late by themselves. It is very important to make sure safety rules are put in place and are followed, because you pissed off a very high-ranking cartel member to be getting threats like this."

The cops arrived at the ranch, and Officer Espinoza met them at the gate. "Dr. Martinez, they are here to escort you to your office now. Are you ready to go?"

"Yes, I guess. As ready as I can be, given what I have been through."

When Dr. Martinez arrived at the office, the cops quickly went through the whole place, checking every window and door and making sure it was clear and no surprises jumped out at them. As the staff arrived, Dr. Martinez called a staff meeting, and he asked Officer Espinoza to conduct the meeting to set in place what he felt was a good buddy system for safety.

During the meeting, Trey had a phone call. The receptionist came into the meeting and said, "Dr. Martinez, your wife is on the phone."

Trey was not looking forward to this call at all. His wife, Lori, had a tendency to get a little worked up and excited. In other words, she panicked about everything.

Trey tried to explain what had happened without giving too much detail, but he was unsuccessful. Lori panicked and demanded to return home. If Lori had any pressure put on her, she would rely on alcohol for comfort. Trey and his wife had serious marriage issues they had been working on, and that was part of the reason why he took the job in McAllen. He kept telling her to stay where she was because she would be safer, but from what others could hear of the conversation, she wasn't having it. "Okay, okay. I'll pick you up at the airport tomorrow." Then he slammed down the phone.

After the meeting, the staff went straight to work alongside Dr. Martinez and finished the clinic as quickly as they could so he could go home and get ready for his wife's arrival. "Okay, guys let's call it a night. The last patient has been seen. See you tomorrow," he said, and he locked the doors after everyone left.

CHAPTER 8

Wow, what a beautiful day. Is it always like this here? Lori was sitting on the back porch, having coffee with her daughter, loving life, and taking it all in before her trip home. Lori looked down at her watch and realized it was later then she thought.

"Hurry, hurry, Jackie. I don't want to miss my flight. I can't wait to get home and see my babies."

Lori called her dogs her babies because Trey and she had kids, but they were grown. All of Lori's spare time was devoted to pampering her dogs.

"I have to be at the airport two hours before the flight to make sure I get my seat."

"Okay, Mom. Calm down. You have plenty of time. It is only a twenty-minute drive to the airport from my house."

Lori loaded her bags in the car, and they set off. As they approached the curb, it looked like it was going to be a full flight, with all the people curbside checking their bags. "Wow, I didn't know that many people lived in this area," she told Jackie, kind of teasing her about her living in the foothills of the Smoky Mountains—and because it was always a bitch to travel there. However, it was a gorgeous place to visit.

"Okay, honey," she said to Jackie, "I have everything. You don't need to stay. I know you are busy with the kids and have your hands full. And besides that, I hate long goodbyes. So give me a hug and know how much I love you and your sister. And know how much I am going to miss you. I promise to come back as soon as I can."

They hugged. "Love you!" Lori yelled as Jackie drove away.

As Lori stood in line, she talked to a gentleman who was traveling to South Texas, and she asked whether he was in the medical field. He replied he was installing some medical equipment at one of the hospitals there and was going to be there for a few days, making sure it operated correctly. She was so excited to learn he was going to McAllen as well. "I hope they seat us together. At least I will have someone to talk to."

He smiled and shook his head. "Yes, that would be great."

After checking in the bags, she hurried to find a place where she could get a quick drink before she boarded. She found a small bar on the concourse. *Great. I can grab a bloody mary because I am not that calm when I fly, and this will help.* She finished one and thought, *I can squeeze one more in before I have to go to the gate. There, that will do it.* She paid her bill, collected her credit card, she headed to the gate.

Lori sat down in one of the empty seats near the gate, waiting for her flight to be called. After twenty minutes, they called for her row to board. She was at the back of the plane because it was such short notice to fly home. She had to fly coach, which meant she was in the second to last row. *Oh well. At least I am one of the first ones to get on the plane,* she thought.

She found her seat, stored all her bags in the overhead compartment, and strapped herself in. Then after another twenty minutes, the pilot came on the radio and announced he was ready for takeoff. Today was a beautiful day for flying: it was clear with no rain and no wind. The temperature was seventy-eight degrees, and the pilot thought the flight would arrive early because the jet stream was running with them.

They were taxied and then were ready to take off, Lori closed her eyes and dozed for fifteen minutes. She thought, *Wow, those drinks really did the trick.* The pilot came on and woke her when he announced they had reached cruising altitude. The flight attendants would be going around with a beverage cart, and people were free to move about the cabin.

Lori thought, *No wonder I saw the flight attendants cutting up limes.* After the announcement, the line to the bathroom became long, spanning several rows in front of her. People were standing and waiting their turn. Lori stood up to stretch her legs, stepped out, and stood in line. By now she remembered those two bloody marys she'd had at the bar because now she needed to use the restroom.

She saw the man whom she had met in line, and he waved at her. He was seated a couple of rows ahead of her. She nodded at him and waved back. He stood up, got in line behind her, and complained about how many people had to use one restroom because the other was marked out of order.

Then he asked, "How is your flight so far? Not scared?"

"No, I am doing great. Just ready to be home."

"That's good," he replied. "I am sure your family misses you."

It was her turn to go in the lavatory. She smiled back at him and locked the door. He stood close to the door and saw he was the last person in line; no one else was behind him. The pilot came on again and asked the flight attendants to prepare for landing because they were thirty minutes out.

Lori opened the lavatory door, and she noticed he was standing so close to the door she could not step out and go around him. The flight attendants were in the front of the cabin and were working their way down the aisle to the back. He looked at one of the attendants and nodded his head at her. She kept the other attendant busy.

When Lori came out, she said, "Excuse me. May I pass?" He said sure, but as she tried to pass him, he grabbed her, covered her mouth, and used a syringe to inject her with a sedative in the neck.

Lori went limp quickly. He took her back inside the lavatory and set her on the floor. While looking down at her, he said, "I am so sorry. I have to do this. As he apologized to her, he stabbed her several times in the abdomen. He took the knife out, washed it, took off his gloves, placed them in a plastic bag, and put them in his pocket. He then exited the lavatory and set the knife in the back where he'd gotten it. The attendant would clean and dispose of it after they landed.

He then looked at the flight attendant and motioned for her to get rid of the knife and anything that was left in Lori's seat showing signs she was there. He switched out the "out of order" sign from the other lavatory and placed it on the outside of the door Lori was in.

He went back to his seat and told the attendant to lock the door from the outside so it would not open. Then he handed her a coffee cup full of hundred-dollar bills with the lid on it. She picked it up, smiled, nodded at the man, said "Gracias," and went about her business.

She cleaned where Lori had been sitting and made sure her bags were tagged to go to the baggage claim when they landed. Now it looked like no one had ever sat there.

After everyone exited the plane, she opened the back entrance for the crew to come aboard, and she handed them the bags to make sure they were sent with the rest of the bags to the baggage claim area. She claimed her personal bag, and the flight attendants and pilots exited the plane as quickly as they could because it was their final destination.

CHAPTER 9

The next morning, Trey got up to the buzzer of the gate. "Hello? Can I help you?"

"Yes, Dr. Martinez I am here to escort you to the airport to meet your wife."

"Oh, yes. How I could forget? I'll buzz you in. Come on up."

He waited at the door till the man rang the doorbell. "Give me a minute. I didn't sleep well last night, and I am not quite awake yet. What time does her plane land?"

"In about thirty minutes, so we will need to get going."

"I need coffee."

"Okay, Doc. We can stop on the way."

"One car or two? I prefer two, but we can go with one. I'll introduce you to my wife. Maybe you can make her feel more comfortable with all the security."

The security official said, "Okay, let's pull out. I'll drive if you don't mind."

Trey was in no position to argue. As they pulled out of the gate, they noticed some stuff on the gate. "Dr. Martinez, I need you to get down. I don't know what's on the gate, but it wasn't there when I arrived earlier. I'm going to go down the road and call someone to go back and check it out. I want you out of harm's way."

Trey agreed. "Let's just get to the airport. I will feel better once she is with us. The flight just landed. Let's go to baggage claim; I told her we would meet her there."

As they sat and waited for all the passengers to arrive in the baggage area, they noticed the passengers had already retrieved their bags and were leaving the airport but, still no Lori. Her bags were the only ones that did not get collected, and the conveyer belt had stopped.

Trey got on the phone right away, but it went straight to voicemail. He went to the reservation desk, but they were limited as to what they would tell him. Finally Trey lost his cool, grabbed an agent, and had the security guard with them explain what had taken place. He had grown concerned because his wife was on this flight but she hadn't gotten off the plane.

The desk agent told them he would page her to see if they got a response. After paging three times, the security with Trey called the detective and let him know what was going on. The police were sending units immediately.

Officer Espinoza arrived and asked airport staff, "Have you started to clean the plane?"

"Yes, we just started."

He asked them to stop, fearing that something had happened to her on the flight. They needed to get on the plane and check.

The guard said, "Follow me, and I will escort you down to the ramp and make sure you have clearance to get onboard and check."

As they got on the plane, they asked Trey to stay at the door in case there was evidence present that needed to be collected. He agreed.

Officer Espinoza checked the bathroom in the front and told the other agent to check the one in the back. As the man approached the door, he could see blood coming from the bottom of the door. "Oh, no. Keep Dr. Martinez in the front unless we need him."

When the detective opened the bathroom door, there was Mrs. Martinez. She was slumped over in a sitting position on the floor.

"Okay, we got her. She is bleeding, and we need an ambulance. She has a faint pulse, but it looks like she was stabbed in the gut. We need to move—now!"

By this time, Trey heard the noise. He ran to the rear of the plane. "Lay her down and let me see how bad the wounds are. I'll see if I can stop the bleeding. Can we get her in the Jetway so I have more room to work on her? That way you guys can make sure no one else is on this plane with us." After a quick examination, he determined that she was stabbed several times in the lower gut and needs surgery immediately.

He called the hospital to put the surgeon on standby so when they got there, they could move quickly to save her life. "The ambulance is here. Let's move." Thank God the hospital is only a few blocks away." Trey could not remember her blood type, and it bothered him because she'd lost a lot of blood.

He told the paramedic to start giving her a bolus of fluid to try to get her of blood volume up. Then he told the security driver to get to the hospital.

As they approached the hospital, Dr. Martinez was pacing and waiting in the emergency entrance for his wife's arrival. When they pulled into the bay, the crew he'd assembled jumped into action. "Get her in here. Let's get her hooked up so we can monitor her vitals. Type and cross her blood, and make sure we have enough. Let's get her a CAT scan so we can see how bad the damage is. Call the operating room and put them on standby. Let's get her moved now. She has several puncture wounds in the lower abdomen and is bleeding out."

Just as they started to move her, the nurse shouted, "BP is dropping!"

Trey said, "She's coded. Start chest compressions. Okay, we are going to shock her. Charging paddles. Clear!" He zapped her chest. "Okay, we have her back for now. Let's go—no time to waste. Where is the surgeon? We don't have time to wait on the CAT scan now. We are going to have to do an exploratory lap to see what the damage is."

"Dr. Martinez, Dr. Alvin is the general surgeon on call, and he is scrubbing in as we speak. He will be ready and waiting on us."

"What about anesthesia?" Already there he was, the first to arrive. "Okay, let's do this. We have to stop the bleeding if we are going to have a chance of saving her life. Let's get her under and open her up."

As they did, they could see the extent of the damage. Two major organs were hit, and there was severe damage to her intestine. She was lucky to be alive; the knife had just barely missed the main artery. Her insides looked like they had gone through a meat grinder. *What a mess. Let's pray we can get this stopped.*

After six hours of surgery, they finally finished.

"Well, Trey, she is alive. But she is not out of the woods."

"Let's get her to ICU. She is going to need someone with her at all times. Don't worry—I will not leave her side. I grant you, this is the most horrendous thing that has ever happened to me or my family. I want someone posted outside the door at all times. No one comes in or out without being checked. Do I make myself clear?"

"Yes, sir, you do."

Trey asked the nurse to get him a cot to sleep on. He let them know he would be staying in her room with her. The nurse asked, "Are you sure you don't want us to make up the bed nearby? And the guard is here."

"No," he said. "I want to be right here in case she wakes up and needs something." Trey glanced down at the blood-covered shirt he was wearing. He closed his eyes and muttered, "I feel so responsible for what has happened to her." He then asked the nurse to get him a pair of scrubs from the surgery department so he could shower, clean up, and put on something clean.

A nurse walked in. "Dr. Martinez, I see you have showered. I hope you feel better. We have your wife's personal belongings; I bagged them. Would you like to hang on to them?"

"Sure. I'll take them to my truck when I leave."

At that time, he looked down and realized his phone was ringing. It was Lori's daughter, Jackie. "Hello, Trey. I have been trying to get hold of Mom. Just wanted to make sure she made it home safe. May I speak with her?"

"Not right now, Jackie. She is taking a shower." Trey made an excuse because he didn't want her daughters to worry—or, God forbid, come down here.

"Can you ask her to call me when she gets a chance?"

"I sure will as soon as she comes out."

"Great. How is she doing?"

"Fine. Everything is good. I'll have your mom call you tomorrow."

Just as he finished up the call, he realized that Officer Espinoza had come into the room. "Smart move, Trey. It is going to be hard enough keeping you two safe. We don't need extra bodies here in the middle of all of this, if we can help it. You need to keep her kids far away from here until this is over. Good night, Trey. I have a guard at the door, and I will check in on you guys in the morning."

Trey put his head down on the bed and closed his eyes, wondering how this got so out of control. He realized he had put his head down on Lori's personal possessions, so he thought, *I'd better go through it and see what's in here.* When he opened the bag, he found Lori's purse and all her jewelry. *Wow that's nice that they thought to keep all of this for me. Lori has quite a bit of a jewelry collection that she wears daily, and it is worth a lot of money.*

Then Trey noticed a piece of paper with some writing on it, tucked in the corner pocket of her purse. Trey opened it, and it read, "I will do to your family what you did to mine."

Trey dropped the note and called Officer Espinoza right away. He told him about what he found tucked into her purse.

"Okay, Trey. Do not touch anything else, and I will come right back and collect the evidence."

Trey thought about his week. Just by going to work one day, he could lose everything, including his family. *Scary. I just have to get my head on straight and see what we have to do to clear this up.* At that moment, he heard a big bang. What is that? He got up to look, and no one was in the hallway. *That's odd. There is supposed to be a guard at all times.* Trey became spooked.

As he made it to the corner, there was a nurse who dropped a monitor and the guard was helping her. "Thank God you are here," the guard responded.

"Yes, sir, I am right here. I heard the noise and just went over to check things out."

"Okay, don't go too far."

"I want to make sure my wife is safe and stays that way."

At that time, all the monitors went off in Lori's room.

The doctor on call said, "Call a code blue! She is in fatal heart rhythm and unresponsive. We are losing her!"

"Charge the paddles!" Trey said.

"Dr. Martinez, I need you to get out of here now and let us do our job. You are interfering and with what we are doing, and we don't have time to fool with you if we are going to save her life."

Trey moved aside and let the crew do their job. He realized he was in no shape to help her right now, so he had to let the doctors and nurses do their job. He felt so helpless, but they were right. He collapsed into a chair at the nearby nurses station, watched from a distance, and prayed for her to regain her life.

"Okay, we have her back, but just barely. This is going to be touch and go. Let's see how she does through the night. If anything changes, page me as soon as you can. I want to stay up on her case. I'll be in the doctor's lounge; I'm going to try to get some sleep."

After Lori was stable, Trey set up the cot to get some sleep. It was going to be a long night after tossing and turning all night.

Trey rolled over and looked at his watch: it was 4:30 a.m. *I might as well get up.* He told the nurse that he was going to the doctor's lounge to eat breakfast. "If you guys need me, page me there." The doctors were always treated to their meals by the hospital, and this morning there was a big spread with coffee, juice, eggs, fruit, and meats.

After choking down what little breakfast he could, he made his rounds with the patients he had admitted. When he finished, he went back to the ICU to check on Lori. "How is she doing?" he asked the nurse.

"She looks good, and it looks like she had a good night and morning. She is holding her own."

"Oh, thank God. That makes me feel a little better I have clinic today, and I need to see some patients and get back to work. I will be out of the building, but my office is almost in the parking lot. Make sure you get hold of me if you need me or if there are any changes—and I mean *any* changes."

"Yes, Dr. Martinez, we will."

CHAPTER 10

D r. Martinez had a full schedule at the clinic, and he welcomed the workload so he could keep his mind busy and not think about the threat he'd gotten from Pablo Cruz. In between patients, Dr. Martinez called to check on Lori. While doing that, he dictated his charts on each patient so his records were always current. At the dictation desk, he became curious about Pablo Cruz, thinking there could not be that much on him. Dr. Martinez had never heard about him, and Pablo had not been in the local news. Dr. Martinez googled him.

"Oh my God."

He read everything that came up on this man, and he could not believe how bad the articles were. They made a lot of accusations but never could get enough evidence to convict him any of the crimes. Every time they had an eyewitness who would testify against him, the witness would die or disappear without a trace.

Just as he finished his research, a nurse came in. "Dr. Martinez, this came for you."

"Okay, put it right here. What is it?"

"I don't know. It is a small cooler with a note on it for you."

He opened the card. It read, "I hope you enjoy," but there was no signature from whoever had sent it. Trey thought nothing of it because they were always ordering new medications for the office or getting gifts of food from the drug reps, so he opened it.

"What the hell! Who sent this to me? Call the cops now! And close the clinic!"

"What is it?"

The detective arrived at the office. They had instructed Trey to not touch anything in the cooler, put the lid back on, and wait for them. "Good afternoon, Dr. Martinez. Where is it? Please leave the room while we open it. Make sure everyone stays safe. Please dismiss your staff and close the clinic for today." All staff was sent home while this took place. Trey looked on cautiously.

Officer Espinoza opened the cooler and said, "Oh my God. I have not seen this in years. Not since the last turf war between the cartels."

In the cooler, there was a folded slab of human skin with a beautiful red bow on it, placed perfectly for display. A note read, "I hope you enjoy."

"Trey, can you come here, please? We need to speak in private. Dr. Martinez, we need to get you out of here as quickly as we can."

"Why? What is it?"

"It is human skin, and it was sent to you as a present. This is a warning that you really need to take it seriously. When the cartel sends you the skin of a human, it is saying, I'm going to do this to you. We need to figure out whom this belongs to. Albert, contact the office and ask if they have found any bodies missing, or any skin in this area."

"Okay, Chief, I'm on it." The chief began watching Albert's face change as he was on the phone. "Okay, I got it, and I will let the chief know."

"Dr. Martinez, let me explain as much as I can so you can get just how serious this is. More than fifty thousand people have been killed since the Mexican government began a crackdown on narcotics trafficking in 2006. Last month, nine bodies were found murdered, tortured, and abandoned outside the mayor's office. The South Texas border towns are an area that houses a vicious feud between the Zeta and the Gulf cartels. We found a banner hanging off the bridge that claimed the victims were a message from the cartel, warning people to be loyal and to not mess with their business or they will end up like this, because this area belongs to them. An all-out turf war is what is going on in our area. All the victims are between twenty-five and thirty years of age, and the cartel claimed full responsibility for all of this, as well as a car bombing outside the police station. Hours later, fourteen headless bodies were found in black garbage bags inside a blue van parked near the market. Just across the border on the Mexican side, drug gangs slaughtered twenty-three more people hanging, nine from another bridge, and fourteen decapitated whose heads were found stashed in coolers near the town hall. Yesterday, another nine bodies were found. Four men and five women were handcuffed and blindfolded, and they bore signs of torture. One body was missing all the skin off of her back, and the cooler they found looks just like the one you got here. They are bought in mass quantity because the cartel uses them to pack their drugs and smuggle them across the border. So, Dr. Martinez, we have a big problem here, and we now we have to make sure you are very careful from here on out."

Trey sat at the desk holding his head while the investigators went through everything in the cooler. One of the detectives approached him and asked, "Are you okay?"

"Yes. I just can't figure out what kind of a person would do something like this."

"A very sick and cruel one, Dr. Martinez."

"How am I ever going to explain this to my family? They are going to be so upset. They have been planning a trip down before my wife and I were due to go on vacation."

"Dr. Martinez, you should contact your family and explain they should not travel here; it is too dangerous, and the trip should be canceled for their safety. But please do not mistake what I am saying. The cartels have long arms and can reach across the United States, if you get what I mean."

Trey's face dropped. "Is she safer here or up there?"

"I can't really answer that. We have seen things happen both ways. Bringing them closer to you could protect them but it could also prove fatal. So could not giving them extra security up where they are. This could prove to be deadly, and they'd be an easy target for revenge if you're not careful. It is your call, Dr. Martinez. Let me know what you decide. I have a private security company on its way. You will need to hire them to be with you twenty-four seven—no exceptions. They will need to post a guard at the office, escort you to and from the hospital, and stay with you while you sleep."

CHAPTER 11

Trey said, "Okay, since I finished the clinic early and have a few patients I need to check on that have been admitted to the hospital, who is going to accompany me there?"

"This is Oscar. He is the best in our area. He doesn't come cheap, but he knows the tricks of the cartel and what they can do, and he is damned good at what he does. I think he is your best chance to survive."

"Okay, Oscar, you are my new best friend. Let's go."

Upon arrival at the hospital, Trey could see lights flashing and cops around a car in the parking lot. They drove up slowly and could see a body behind the wheel of the car, slumped over the seat. Trey rolled the window down and asked, "What happened?"

"One of the people standing around answered, "A nurse is the victim of a drive-by shooting." "Really? Which nurse?"

"Janie from OB."

Trey hit his breaks. Oscar asked, "What's wrong?"

"The nurse. Oh my God, the nurse!"

"What about the nurse?"

"I worked with her the other night, trying to save that lady and her baby. That one from Mexico with the husband who threatened me."

"Did she have any contact with Pablo Cruz?"

"Oh my God, yes. She worked directly with him about the procedure and what was going to happen. Do you think the staff in the operating room is in danger?"

"Your family and anyone who had contact with Pablo Cruz or his bodyguards are in danger. Let me check the area of the shooting, because if it was Cruz, there will be a calling card." Oscar pulled his gun and said, "Let's get you inside the hospital quickly."

"What's wrong? What did you see?"

"We don't have a lot of help here, and you are out in the open. Dr. Martinez, it is so important that you do what I tell you. When you get inside the hospital, don't leave my sight. This hospital is very big and has a lot of hiding places. Anyone could be working for or with Cruz. Yes, I am sorry, Dr. Martinez. It is Janie from OB, and there was a calling card pinned to her chest."

"What did it say?"

"I have no idea yet. Let's get you inside."

CHAPTER 12

D r. Martinez parked his car, and they sprinted across the hospital parking lot. When they got inside, they were stopped by security.

"Good evening. I guess you saw what happened outside?"

"Yeah, I did."

"What happened? Was it a boyfriend or ex-husband?"

"No, sir. You need to come with me. Detective Espinoza is here and wants to speak with you. Come this way."

As Dr. Martinez entered the room, he could see on the detective's face that this was not good. "Good evening. I'm sorry we have to keep meeting this way."

"What does this have to do with me, other than Janie and I worked together on Pablo Cruz's wife and child?"

"Nothing, Trey, until we found a note in the car attached to the body. It was addressed to you."

Trey's face turned pale, and he stumbled. "I'm in the business of saving lives, not taking lives. This is crazy. What did the note say?"

"Just the same thing as he said to you: 'I will do to you what you did to my family.' The girl was shot at close range. She didn't have a chance, and the note was there."

"Did she have a family?"

"Yes, two kids and a husband. There is one more thing, Dr. Martinez. She is missing two fingers that look like they have been cut off tonight."

Trey responded, "I think I am going to be sick."

"We will have to check and see if they were amputated before she died or after."

Trey responded, "What difference does it make now that she is dead?"

"It will tell us if she was tortured before death."

"This is all my fault. How am I ever going to face these people here again? I am so disgusted." Trey realized the situation was escalating and not getting any better. The detective suggested Trey take some handgun classes and wear a gun on his hip at all times, so they went to do the instructional class with the cops and took their advice. Trey bought a pistol and a holster for the hip. This was great for outside the hospital, but they didn't allow any guns on the premises or while he was in the operating room unless it was security. "We are going to have to post security outside the operating room while you are working. Do I need to clear this with administration? We don't want any new problems."

After working about ten hours straight delivering babies and doing surgeries, Dr. Martinez decided to call it a night. It was about eleven o'clock in the evening, and he was exhausted. He called off the crew and said he was heading to his wife's room to spend the night with her. He called the ranch to make sure the caretaker of the property was okay and to see whether everything was good on the home front.

"Alberto, is everything okay out there on the ranch?"

"Yes, yes, everything is good. But I have to ask—how is Ms. Lori? Please let her know my wife and I have been praying for her speedy recovery. My wife tidied up the house today and washed the porch where the pooch was. I buried her in the back; I can show you when you get home. My wife is a little spooked being out here. We have worked on this ranch for sixteen years, even before you bought it, and we have never seen anything like this before. Do you mind if we go to our daughter's house tonight? We would also like to take the next couple of days off. I will leave her there and then come back."

"Sure, Alberto. I am so sorry for all of this. I am sure you guys are not that comfortable there right now. Hopefully, this will be over soon. Make sure you put out enough feed and hay for a couple of days for the animals, and then go ahead and leave."

"I will, and I'll see you in a couple of days."

"Make sure you call me and let me know when you're coming back."

"I sure will, Dr. Martinez. You take care, amigo."

"Adios."

As Trey finished his call, he sat and looked at Lori. Now in her forties, she was a thin-faced woman who'd lost her glow long ago. He remembered the life he'd shared with her prior to him working so much. She had been so full of life and so carefree, the most beautiful, charismatic blue-eyed woman he had ever seen. Now, he didn't know whether she was even going to make it.

They'd met in college. Both had had short, failed marriages, but once they connected, it was like they were thunderstruck. They had vowed to never be apart again.

Trey whispered to her, "I don't want to play games with our marriage any longer, Lori. I realize how much I love and need you in my life. Whatever our problems are, we will get through them; I promise. You just have to hang on, fight, and get well."

Lori could only hear half of what Trey was saying. Her eyes blinked open and closed several times, and she drew a deep breath. He saw tears had formed in her eyes. She said, "I wasn't sleeping. I can hear you."

"Lori! I can't believe you are awake."

She responded, "Where am I?"

"You are in the hospital. I am just so thankful you are awake."

"Hospital? What happened?"

"I guess you don't remember much, do you?"

"No, not much."

"Well, that really doesn't matter right now." Trey reached across the bed, his muscles rigid and taut in his arms. He strained to catch every word she was trying to say. Speaking softly and weak, she looked up at him and said, "I would invite you into the bed with me, but there is not much room."

"Oh, Lori, I love you, and I am so happy you still have your sense of humor after all you have been through."

"I love you too, Trey."

"Please rest—you need it. Let me get the nurses so they can check you out." He ran to the desk and got the nurse, but by the time he returned, she was out again. "She was just talking to me, and her eyes were open."

The nurse responded, "You know, they can do that and never regain consciousness. Just be patient and talk to her. She seems to respond to that, and she is a very strong-willed lady." The nurse finished checking her vitals and said, "Everything looks good. If you need anything else, please let me know."

"Okay, I will." Trey was disappointed he didn't get to talk to her much, but he was grateful for the few words. He put his head down, and when he did, he fell fast asleep. He was exhausted.

CHAPTER 13

Trey woke up the next morning to find out that he'd slept hard and hadn't heard a thing all night long. When he pulled himself together, he looked out the door to make sure security was still in place and to his liking. It was. "Thank God," he mumbled under his breath as he nodded at the guard.

"Good morning, Dr. Martinez. Did you sleep well? I made sure the nurses didn't wake you when they went in and out of the room."

"I slept pretty well because I heard nothing. Thank you for that. I needed the rest. When is your replacement due to be here this morning?"

"Anytime now is the shift change. I'll make sure he checks in with you when he gets in here."

"Okay. I'm going to shower, but I need to go to my house to get a fresh change of clothes before I start my day at the clinic."

Trey waited on the new security to arrive, but he started losing his patience with them because it was not happening fast enough for him. Trey was not one to sit around and do nothing. He had always been known as the workhorse, and he always had a full schedule and needed to do rounds before he started his surgeries at two o'clock in the afternoon—and before that, he had the morning clinic.

After about twenty minutes of waiting, he told the guard outside the door, "I can't do this, so you are to stay with my wife until the replacement arrives." He told him he was heading to his house for fresh clothes. The guard insisted on him waiting for the bodyguard, but Trey shrugged his shoulders and said, "I don't have time for this, and he is late. Be sure you tell him what I am doing so he can catch up with me after I shower, shave, and change my clothes. I'm going by my office for just a few hours, and then I am heading back here."

Trey hopped in his car and headed out the gate. After pulling out, he realized he hadn't eaten anything, and he was starving. *I'll hit my favorite taco place to get breakfast.* He laughed to himself about his eating habits and then felt bad because he was making fun of his wife, who was hurt. He thought, *She doesn't need to know what I'm having for breakfast.* He ordered his breakfast tacos and waited in line, thinking about what had been happening these past few days and how crazy it had been. He was so engrossed in his thoughts that the line moved and he wasn't even aware of it till the guy behind him honked to let him know. "Sorry, buddy," he said as he waved out the window. After getting his food and heading to the ranch, like always he couldn't resist digging into the tacos. He seemed to be in a fairly good mood. "Oh my," he said while he was eating and driving, laughing to himself. He thought, *I don't know what in the world they do to these, but they are delicious. Lori can't make them taste like this, not even close.*

As Trey arrived at the ranch, he finished eating his tacos so he could start paying close attention to everything and make sure nothing looked suspicious. *So far, so good. The dogs ran right to my truck.* Trey parked the truck and got out. "Hi, babies. I sure have missed you guys."

The dogs came running and jumping all over him, happy to see him. Trey head to the house and thought about what the detective had told him about safety. He placed his alarm button in one of his hands and his gun in the other. He walked up on the porch and saw nothing out of the ordinary, so he went inside. *House looks good. Lori would be happy; everything is spick-and-span.* He made his way to the bedroom and walked into the master bath that led to the closet.

He opened the drawers to get fresh clothes, and there it was. "Oh shit!" he screamed. "Oh, how sick is this?" In the drawer were two severed fingers, and when Trey looked closer, he could tell they belonged to a woman. He recognized the decoration on one of them because it had been shown to him a few days earlier. "Oh my God. They belong to Janie. Oh my God! Oh my God!" He reached for his cell phone and realized he had left it in the kitchen. Shaking all over, he ran back to the kitchen, squatted down, and placed a call to the guard and to the police. He explained to the detective, "Get here as quick as you can. I think I have Janie's fingers."

"What?"

"Just what I said. Some sick son of a bitch put Janie's fingers in my drawer of clothes at my house."

"Okay, we are en route, Dr. Martinez. Be careful—they could still be on the property. Stay in one spot away from the windows."

"Okay. The gate code is 6543. Hurry!"

Trey squatted down and felt sick at his stomach. He called the dogs to come to him because he knew they would raise the alarm if someone came up. The dogs stayed with him and did not move or make a sound. He thought, *I'm either going to die and you guys know it, or you guys are really happy to see me, are scared shitless as well, and don't want me to leave.*

When he picked his head up, he could see lights flashing at the gate from the cops. It was a great relief to see the cavalry coming. Trey took a deep breath, released it, and said to himself, "I don't know how much more I can take of this."

Detective Espinoza came up to the door. "Dr. Martinez, where are you?"

"Over here." Trey stood up, weak in the knees. "Thank God you are here. This one was a true scare. I thought I was a dead man and they were still in the house with me. I am still shaking."

"Sit down over here and compose yourself. Let's go through what happened. Okay, who is upstairs?"

"No one that I know of. We never go up there unless we have company."

Detective Espinoza motioned to the other policemen to go upstairs and check it out.

"It is all clear now," they shouted down the stairs. "But it looks like someone has been staying up here. There are food and drinks up here."

"That's strange, because the maid just told me she had cleaned everything to get it ready for Lori when she comes home."

"Well, it even looks like someone was lying on the bed."

"This is crazy! I have an alarm on the house. How did they get in?"

Espinoza said, "That is the easy part. If they have access to someone who works with the alarm company, or they have someone watching you, or they know your caretaker and his wife. Those are the only options." He turned to one of his men. "Let's look at the alarm."

"Okay, Chief, I'm on it."

After about fifteen minutes, the man came back and said, "Chief, I know what happened. The alarm has been cut and deactivated. All the wires are hanging out of the box. You can check it out, if you like."

As he finished with his sentence, he looked at Officer Espinoza and said, "We have another issue. If you come with me, I can show you."

Officer Espinoza got up and followed him outside to the back of the house. "What do you need?"

"Chief, please look in the pool. Just below the waterfall."

"Oh shit. I see it. What kind of a person would do this? Has the doctor seen this yet?"

"No, not yet."

"Okay. Call the crime team and get them to the back of the house so we can get this taken care of."

In the bottom of the pool, just below the waterfall so it was hard to see, was a severed human head.

"We are going to need to get it out of the pool and see if the doctor knows him. After you get it out, let me know. I am going back inside to see if we have any more surprises." Espinoza reentered the house. "Okay, Trey, we have another problem in the backyard, but I don't want you to go out there until they call us back there and have gathered all the evidence they need."

"What in the hell is going on, Espinoza?"

"I'll tell you. Sit down and don't freak out. There is a part of a person in your pool."

"What? What part of a person?"

"A head, Dr. Martinez. A person's head."

"Are you kidding me?"

"I wish I was. They are in the process of getting it out. I don't want you walking around out there until it is clear."

Trey's mouth fell open. "Who is it?"

"We don't know yet. We are going to bag it and then let you take a look to see if you can help us out with his identity."

Trey's face turned white, and he said, "I think I am going to be sick."

"Bend over, Doc, and catch your breath. We are going to need you in just a few minutes."

As Trey was sitting there, the young officer came to the door. "Officer Espinoza, we are ready for you."

"Okay, Trey, we need to go out to the pool. Let's go."

Just as Trey walked out, the young officer approached and said, "Over here. We are ready for the doctor."

They unzipped the bag, and Trey said, "Oh no! I know who he is, but I don't know him. I just met him the other night. This is the driver of the dead woman and child. I met him at the hospital when I was trying to get some information from him about the patient. I think he was the one who brought her to the hospital, and he said he worked for her husband, Pablo Cruz." He looked at Officer Espinoza and told him, "I am not pleased with the way this whole investigation has been going. It seems like no progress is being made to stop this man. "I am not going to stand by and let this asshole murder me and my family. You guys have to do something. You run around like you know how to handle this, and yet this man keeps getting access to my home, my office, and my life. I'm not going to just sit by anymore! You guys had better figure this out, and quickly, because I am getting fed up with this crap."

Trey stormed out, got in his truck, and sped off. On the way to the gate, he looked at the pasture with his cattle in it and thought something was a little off. He hit his brakes, came to complete stop, turned around, and went back to the house. "Officer Espinoza, can you come over here? You guys see the left pasture?"

"What about it?"

"There is something on fire out there."

All the cops went running to the field, and they yelled to call the fire department because whatever was burning needed to be put out quickly. There was a stick on fire, and the stick had a shoe on it. "Hurry. We want to get whatever or whoever it is out of the flames."

As they approached the area, the flames went higher, and they could clearly see a person in the flames. "Oh God, who is that?" The fire department arrived and put out the flames, and they got the body to stop burning. When they looked, they asked, "Dr. Martinez do you know him?"

Trey looked and said in a somber tone, "I'm really not sure—he is almost unrecognizable." Just as Trey turned to leave, he looked down and could see something that looked a little familiar. "The shoe," he said. "I know that shoe."

"Okay, to whom does it belong?"

"Me," Trey responded. "That is a pair of my old shoes that I gave to my caretaker so he had an extra pair for the ranch. That is my old shoe. God, please tell me this is not happening. But if he was wearing the shoes, this has to be Alberto."

"How and when did this happen? And his truck is not here that I can see. Is there any place on the ranch that is more secluded?"

"Yes, let's get in my truck, drive back to the creek, and see if his truck is there." Trey drove them around the property and finally came upon Alfredo's truck. "There it is. That is the ranch truck he uses."

They all piled out and went up to the vehicle. After looking inside, they could see there had been a struggle, and blood was all over the seat. "Call the crime scene investigators. We need them back here again."

As the team arrived, Detective Espinoza stayed close to Dr. Martinez. "I have a bad feeling about this, Trey. I feel like we are being watched as we are working here. This is like being a human target and I am waiting to be shot."

"Okay, Detective, I think we have all we can get for now. I am going to remove the truck from the property and move it to the lab for further testing. It looks like someone walked up on Alfredo while he was sitting in the truck, and it started from there. I don't see any bullets, but with the amount of blood in that truck, I would not put it past being a stabbing."

"Was the head intact?"

"We could not tell; the body was too burned. As soon as I get it back to the lab, I will be able to tell you. Have you guys notified the next of kin?"

"No, not yet. I want to make sure it is him before we contact his family."

CHAPTER 14

Trey looked at the team of people at the house and said, "I have to get out of here. I can't stand this, and I feel like I am a sitting duck. I'm going to grab a hotel room and stay part of the night thereafter I see my wife."

Trey went to his truck, got in, and left as the detective yelled at him to let them know where he was going to be. He drove off and thought, *I need security with me. I will have to get security at the hospital to meet me in the parking lot.* But then he had a second thought. *I have never run from anything in my life, and I am not going to start now.* On his way to the hospital, he realized he had some new instruments at the office that came in, and he needed to get them to the operating room to be sterilized for the surgeries on tomorrow's schedule. Usually his tech took them up there for him. *It's too dangerous at this time, so I will grab them on my way.* He parked right at the front door of his office, went in, and locked the door behind him.

As he went through the office messages and mail that had been piled on the front desk, he sat in the office and thought, *How in the world has this happened? My friends are dead, my wife is barely alive, and now an employee is dead because he worked for me. This man is pure evil. What am I going to do to get a handle on this?* He thought about giving in to Pablo Cruz and saying, "Here I am. Let me take whatever you want to do to me." But after remembering all the horrific acts he'd read about online, he decided it was not a smart idea. In reality, he couldn't give up. A lot of people depended on him and needed him to make them well so they could take care of their families. He thought, *Wow, the office is backed up. Look at all the patients I have neglected. But everyone is too scared to come to work and be around me for fear of getting hurt. I don't blame them because I don't like being here either, by myself. It is a sad place right now. This place is usually teaming with patients and life.*

Trey heard something in the waiting room. He stood and looked around but found nothing. It was a big office with a lot of exam rooms, and his office was in the back for privacy. He went back to doing what he'd been doing. Then when he looked up, he saw the door close. "Hello? Is anyone there?" No one replied. Trey got up and looked around, but he saw nothing. He had a gut feeling that something was wrong. He went through every room but found nothing. It still felt creepy in there, so Trey finally decided to call his security guard. He grabbed his phone and dialed.

"Hello, this is Dr. Martinez. Where are you? I haven't seen much of you today."

"I'm actually pulling up in your parking lot as we speak."

"Oh, thank God. Something weird is going on in here."

"Officer Espinoza called me and told me to track you down. You see, Dr. Martinez, if I can find you this easily, so can they. I'll be right there."

Trey took a deep breath and exhaled with relief. "I'm so glad you are here. I think my mind is playing tricks on me."

"Well, you have been through a lot of trauma, Dr. Martinez. I sure you are questioning everything and hearing all kinds of things in there. When this building is empty, it echoes."

Trey went to the front entrance to let him in, and again he found the door open. "This is crazy. I know I locked it because I left my keys hanging in the door."

The bodyguard entered the office and said, "Dr. Martinez, you okay? You look like you saw a ghost. Your keys were hanging on the outside of the door. Here, let me get them."

"I'm good," Trey replied. "Let's just get out of here."

Trey's office was located just a few blocks from the hospital, and he took great comfort in getting into a public building with people and not being alone.

CHAPTER 15

"Hang on, Dr. Martinez. I'll walk you upstairs. Okay, let's go." As they moved through the front entrance, they heard over the intercom, "Code blue, ICU. Code blue, ICU."

"Oh no!" Trey yelled. "That could be Lori! Let's go. I have my badge to get us in. Come on!"

As they arrived, it was Lori as the code blue, but the clerk stopped Trey at the door and would not let him in. "What happened?" he asked.

"I don't know, Dr. Martinez. All I know is they told me to catch you at the door and not let you in until it was over."

Trey started pacing back and forth, yelling at the nurses and doctors in the room. Trey knew this couldn't be good. Finally, one of the nurses emerged from the room, and he asked what had happened.

The nurse told him his wife's heart went into cardiac arrest. "We have been working on her for an hour already, and they are going to have to call it before too long."

"No!" Trey yelled, and he punched the wall. "This can't be happening to me."

Just as he turned, the doctor came out of the room and said, "Dr. Martinez, I am so sorry, but your wife didn't make it. We did everything we could, but she is gone.

Is there someone we can call for you?"

"No. I just want to go and see her."

Trey sat beside her bed, and he broke down and cried. "I am so sorry," he said. "I am so sorry. You deserved so much better than me and this."

Trey looked at his bodyguard and told him, "I don't know what to do or where to go. She was my life. Regardless of how badly we would fight, I always knew I had her by my side. And now she is gone." Trey stayed with her for about thirty minutes.

The nurse came in and said, "Dr. Martinez, the morgue is here to take the body. Do you have a preference for a funeral home? Would like me to call for you?"

"No. Just pick a nice one and let me know which one. I'm going to get a hotel room and make some calls. I need to call her kids before they hear about it through friends and family." As Trey left the room, he told the bodyguard, "I'm not going to need your services any longer. Send your time into the bookkeeper at my office, and they will cut a check for you. I can't do this any longer."

The guard said, "Wait, you can't do this. They will hurt you."

Trey responded, "I don't care. I have nothing left to live for."

Trey went to the hotel and made one of the most dreadful phone calls, letting her kids know their mom had passed away. He was Devastated and sad. "This is the worst day of my life. I'm so sorry to have to tell you this, Jackie, and I really don't know how to say it, but here goes. You mom passed away today."

"No! Not Mom! I just saw her yesterday. What happened? "How did this happen? What the fuck is going on, Trey?" Jackie never minced words; one could always count on her to get straight to the point.

Trey sat on the phone for an hour going over everything that had happened. Then he also explained he wanted a private funeral to be held in the city that the girls were in, not here for safety reasons. "I don't want you guys to travel down here or have to go out of your way when it is just me here."

Lori's daughter fell to pieces and wept. "She was everything to me, Trey. I don't understand. I just don't get what happened. Mom was fine when she boarded the plane to go back home."

"I know," Trey kept telling her. "There is a lot more to this, but I am not going to explain this over the phone. Let me get the funeral home squared away, and I will fly up with her tomorrow. We can go over everything, and I will try to explain everything to you guys. Please contact a funeral home, and have them meet us at the plane. I don't want anything big, just family."

"All right, Trey. I've got it. I don't understand, but okay."

After Trey hung up the phone, he broke down and cried. He couldn't believe he'd lost his Lori like this, in such a painful way. *I blame myself for this.* He remembered how Lori did not want to move down here; she'd called it a third-world country in parts. *I forced her into it. If we had just stayed in Dallas, this would not have happened.* Trey was not a big drinker, but tonight was one of those nights where he needed to blow off some steam and try to put this out of his mind. He could not stop himself, and he drank until he passed out.

The next morning, Trey woke to a knock at the door. "Dr. Martinez, it's Officer Espinoza. I came by to check on you." When Trey opened the door, Officer Espinoza looked at him and said, "Must have been one rough night."

"What do you want?"

"You look like shit. I am here to make sure you are okay. Here is your morning paper. Your wife made the front page."

"Yeah, I'm great, can't you tell?" Eager to return to the bed and sleep off his hangover, Trey knew he couldn't look at Officer Espinoza. "Come in. I need to take a shower."

"I know this has been hard on you, Trey, but you have to keep it together if you are going to survive. What's your plan?"

"Well," Trey said, "today I get to go pay the funeral home for preparing my wife and transporting her wife to North Carolina for her private service. Then I'm going to fly up there for the service and stay a couple of days. After that, I am going to return and put everything I have left here up for sale. And I am getting the hell out of here and never looking back. I am not living like this, and if I had known it was this different down here, I would have never come."

Officer Espinoza stood there and said, "I understand, Trey. I would feel the same way. I am so sorry this happened to you. But there are still a lot of good things that happen down here as well. It's not all bad. Let me know when you are ready to go. I want to drive you and make sure you are safe on the plane."

Trey's mouth was still parched, and he said, "Give me an hour to shower, clean up, and get coffee."

Officer Espinoza replied, "You shower, and I will go get coffee for you. I'll be back in an hour, so get yourself ready."

Trey agreed.

CHAPTER 16

Officer Espinoza arrived with the coffee and commented, "Trey, you look a little more presentable. Not clean-shaven, but showered. How's the head? I also brought you some aspirin."

"Oh, thank you," Trey responded. "But I feel like shit, and feel like I am in a damned dream and haven't woke up yet."

"I know, buddy. This has to be hard. I am going to stay with you until you get on that plane, so let's go. I'm driving."

"Hey, I need to ask you a question. How did you find me?"

"That's my job, Trey: finding people. And you are easy—you leave a paper trail all over the place." Trey got in the car. Officer Espinoza asked, "Which funeral home?"

"It is Legacy, on Twenty-Third Street. They are getting everything ready for me."

"Okay, let's go."

On the way there, Trey sat stone-faced and had very little to say; they drove in silence. They arrived at the funeral home, and the director met them at the door. "This way, Dr. Martinez. I have everything ready for you. You said not to spare any expense on the casket. We prepared the body. I hope you approve."

Trey looked at the love of his life and broke down. "She looks so beautiful and peaceful, like she is sleeping and everyone is waiting for her to wake up. This will be fine. Just tell me what I owe you, and let me get on my way."

"Are you flying commercially?"

"No. I chartered a place small, a G6, waiting for us on the tarmac."

"I want that plane up in the air as soon as I make sure it is safe for you. Please load the body so we can get it to the plane."

The hearse followed them to the plane, and the gates opened for them to pull directly up to the plane. They loaded the body, and Officer Espinoza told him he would check on the property and feed the dogs for Trey, but when he looked inside, the dogs were kenneled and on board for the flight. "These two dogs were Lori's babies. I can't take a chance of them getting hurt or losing them as well. One of my friends went to the ranch and got them for me."

"Okay, Dr. Martinez. Everything checks out, and you are good to board and take off."

Trey got onboard, and they shut the door. The pilot said, "Buckle up for a fast takeoff. It's going to be a quick trip down the runway before we are airborne. I'm trying to beat some bad weather heading in. Once we are up, you can move around freely. The weather is bad, and we may have to go around it. Trey knew it had to be bad because Officer Espinoza had told him to take off as soon as he boarded.

The plane taxied and, it was one of the quickest takeoffs Trey had ever been on. As soon as they were airborne and at cruising altitude, Trey started to cry. He said to his wife, "I never thought this would be our last flight together." The dogs whimpered as they lay next to her casket.

CHAPTER 17

The service was beautiful and small, just like Trey wanted, with as many flowers as the chapel could hold; Lori would have approved. The family was heading to the car when Jackie asked Trey, "What you are going to do?"

He spent hours telling them what had happened with the patient and what he'd thought had happened to their mom. "I asked her to stay up here with you guys, but you know how hard-headed she can be."

Jackie responded, "Yes, Mom was very headstrong."

"I am so sorry, and I miss her so much. I am going back to put everything up for sale—the house, the practice, all of it. I have movers ready to pack up the house as soon as I get there. I am not going to get rid of anything that belonged to your mom. I am going to move it back to our place in Dallas, and you guys can come over there and pick out the stuff you want. But do *not* come to the Valley! It is not safe! I could not handle going through this with either of you"

CHAPTER 18

Trey landed in McAllen, and Espinoza was waiting on him.

"Hello, Officer Espinoza. Thank you for the flowers you sent to the service. They were beautiful. Well, did you miss me?"

"Yes, Trey. I haven't had a pain in the butt to work with this past week—but you are here now. Just kidding. What's on the agenda for today?"

"I need to go by my house, pick up some things, and get my truck. Then I am heading to my office. I can never seem to make it there before bad things happen, so hopefully today will be a good day."

"Okay, I'll go with you."

"Great, I would appreciate that. Yes, I have a full day at the office today. Because I've been gone, I have to make it up to my patients."

"I am sure they understand, with the passing of your wife. That's pretty significant."

"I am going to put the practice up for sale, and the hospital is looking at my contract with them to see if we can work out something to let someone else take over the practice. We'll work out all the financial stuff. Some of my patients won't like changing doctors in the middle of pregnancy, but we will simply have to work through it. My heart aches. Let's get going and get this over with."

"I'll wait for you outside, Trey. I checked the house a few hours ago, and while you were gone it has been very quiet. I want to walk the property before we leave, just to make sure. Without your pups, it's quiet out here."

"Yeah, I know. That's why I took a suite at the hotel until I can get all of this gone. The movers will be here tomorrow."

CHAPTER 19

When Trey arrived at the office, it was jammed packed with patients, Flowers, plants, and food were everywhere. The staff was there and ready to work. "Wow what is all of this?" Trey said. "Patients, friends, and family have loaded the office with all of this. This is overwhelming, it is going to make me cry. I'll be in my office for a few minutes to pull myself together. Let me know when the first patient is ready."

Later, Trey said, "Okay, let's get started. We have ninety-eight patients today, and we will be here late, so I hope you guys are ready." After seeing the first few patients Trey got back in the swing of things, and it was like he had never been gone. Trey the workhorse was back. Most patients were very responsive and glad to see him, and they trusted him with their and their babies' lives.

"Dr. Martinez, the next patient is ready. We have five more before lunch."

"Okay, Leti. I want to order in. Leave that food for the staff. Just order something hot for me and bring it into my office; I don't want to go anywhere."

"There is a lot of food here already. Go look, and if you want something different, let me know."

"Just order me something, please." Trey was very surprised no one had mentioned the lady who had passed away, but they offered many condolences for his wife.

Trey wondered how Mia's family was doing and if the service had already happened for her and the baby. He wanted to send flowers or something to the service, but it was held in Mexico, and he didn't know how his action be taken. He wondered if her husband was still mad at him and blamed him for the loss of his family, or whether he finally considered them even. He often caught himself thinking that if she had been his patient from the beginning, this would not have happened. He could have stopped it long before all of this happened. Letting this go so far was a travesty, and Lori had suffered because of it. Her death was heart-wrenching.

Trey was very careful and took extra time with all his patients, making sure no complications were arising. He thought, *I never again want to go through what I just did with Mia, with one of my patients.* It was seven o'clock in the evening, and after a long, grueling day, the work was finally finishing up. Trey became aware that he had nowhere to go but to the hotel. There was no way he could ever go back to the house he'd shared with Lori. They'd worked so hard on it to put it back together and make it their dream home. The property was empty and had sat vacant for several years before Trey and Lori had purchased it. It had been rundown and in bad shape, and now it would be lost forever.

Trey realized all his dreams and hard work were totally lost without his wife, and he was miserable. *I am going to eat and get back to work at office dictations. I'll work as much as I can to keep my mind from wandering and speculating on what would have been if Lori had made it—and to keep from worrying about Pablo Cruz.*

The last of the patients had finished, and the staff was on their way out. "Can I get you anything else before I leave, Dr. Martinez?"

"Did you put the patient files on my desk that I asked for?"

"Yes, sir. I did all the files that you have not dictated. They are there along with the others. Is there anything else?"

"No, I guess not. Just lock me in. I'm going to finish these charts and then catch some sleep. Thanks for everything, Leti. I could not have gotten through this day without all of you guys."

"You bet, sir. We are just glad you are back. See you tomorrow."

"Good night."

After two charts Trey's mind started to wander. *There is no way I can concentrate. Maybe this was a bad idea. What if we had not moved here? What if I had not been on call? What if, what if, what if. That is all that occupies my mind. The guilt is overwhelming.* He sat back, finished his meal, closed his eyes, and put his head down on his desk. Just for an instant, he thought he could hear his wife calling him. When he opened his eyes, he thought, *This is crazy. I know she is gone. My mind must be playing tricks on me.* But it was so peaceful and calming and as clear as a bell. *I would do anything to hear her voice again or see her alive and vivacious.*

Trey thought, *I must be losing my mind.* He started charting again and doing his dictations. All of a sudden, glass came crashing down in the waiting room. *What the hell?* He ran in the front to look around but saw no one. He ran for the phone, but when he picked it up, it was dead. *Oh no. What is going on?* Then he saw a shadow run across the back of the office—and it ran directly behind him. Trey closed his eyes. He knew it was his time; they had already gotten everyone else who was involved in the delivery of Mia's baby and had tried to save their lives, and now it was his time.

He yelled, "I know you are there. Just show yourself!" No response. "Please just show yourself, and let's get this over with. I can't live like this any longer, looking over my shoulder and around every corner just to make sure no one is in the room with me. That is not supposed to be."

As he turned around, he saw Detective Espinoza and said, "Oh, thank God it is you. I thought I was going nuts and someone else was with me."

Officer Espinoza responded, "I had not had the chance to see you today. "You look like you're losing it a little, Trey. You need to get out of here, take a shower, and get some sleep. Everything will be better for you in the morning. They told me you were here, so I thought I would pop in on you. When I drove up, I heard a loud noise and saw someone running from the back of your office, so I followed the person as far as I could. The culprit sped off in a truck. Are you okay?"

"Yes, I'm fine. Just a little shaken up."

"What happened?"

"I was working late, and I heard a noise and saw busted glass all over the front waiting room."

When Officer Espinoza went into the front waiting area to check out everything, he was relieved no one was in the office with them. "We are all clear. No one is here. It's okay, Dr. Martinez. They just broke out the front windows." After looking around Officer Espinoza saw the bullets in the wall. "Looks like someone was trying to scare you. They drove by and shot the windows. Thank goodness you and your staff were not in the front of the office—you might be dead."

Trey walked around to the front and could not believe what he saw. "Officer Espinoza, I don't know what to do anymore. This is getting so out of hand. I thought this would be over by now. I was gone for a few days, and nothing happened. Now that I return, it picks right back up."

"Well, Trey, you are the last one from the operating room who encountered Mr. Cruz, so we have to concentrate on keeping you safe and out of sight. I want to remind you they never seem to forget. Maybe you should consider shutting down the practice, taking some time off, and going up with your family. Let this die down. Do you think that would help?"

"I really don't know, but I do know they have long arms and can touch you anywhere. Maybe you are better off here so that we can keep an eye on you. I really don't know what to tell you."

"I have to work, Trey explained. "People depend on me for their jobs and for their health."

"It's your call to let me know what you want. I need to call someone to come and board up the office windows.

Then tomorrow I can get the glass replaced. Let me know when you are ready to leave, and I will escort you to the hotel tonight."

"If I wait, they could do it now, and they should be here in twenty minutes. After they are finished, we can leave."

After the guys finished boarding up the office, Trey got in his truck, and Officer Espinoza followed him to make sure he was safe. When they got to the hotel, Trey met Officer Espinoza in the hotel lobby. Espinoza explained to Trey how important it was for him to check everything and to stay with him.

Trey was frustrated with the way he had to live his life, and he told the officer he didn't need his services anymore. "I can't do this. I'm going to shut it down, take a leave of absence from the hospital staff, and go away for a while. I'm going to get my schedule cut down to two days, and I'm out of here."

"Dr. Martinez, I would not advise you to do this. I have already called the crew to be at the hotel with you until morning, and they will stand watch through the night."

Trey reluctantly agreed. "I just want to go shower and lie down." All he could think about was Lori and how alone he felt. He remembered what a lucky man he was and how everyone liked Lori. He'd known the minute he'd laid eyes on her: he'd fallen in love. When they were in school, she'd been loved by everyone. She'd had a great personality and gotten along with everyone. *Her looks—oh my gosh. How I miss looking at those beautiful, seductive blue eyes. And that golden blonde hair with a body to die for, perfect tone and in shape, with a little nip and tuck done periodically to help her with the aging of her skin.* He loved it when she would lock eyes on him. He knew her eyes would pierce his heart and make it flutter. With a cute little crooked smile, she would lay her cheek on his chest, and the chest hair would always tickle her nose. What he missed the most was the passion she had every time she planted a deep, erotic kiss on his lips. He groaned and thought about the time he'd taken her on their first date. He met her gaze and told her straight out he was going to marry her—right after he got through fucking her.

After several minutes of pleasuring himself, he left the bed and went into the bathroom. He didn't turn on any lights and moved by feel through the doorway. He found the sink and fresh washcloths. He waited a few minutes for the water to get warm and washed himself. After finishing, he broke down, dropped to his knees, and cried like a baby. Lori and Trey had a love-hate relationship. When it was good, it was great; when it was bad, he hated being in the same room with her. She was a recovering alcoholic, and he had a hard time dealing with her.

The hospital had a welcoming dinner for them at the hospital, and she excused herself from the table to go to the powder room and never came back. Dr. Martinez looked around the room and finally spotted her. She was on the other side of the room, and when he got up to escort her to the table, she said she had gotten lost and couldn't find him. She was so drunk he could hardly understand her speech. He knew it was time to leave the dinner before someone noticed. He escorted her out by the waist and never let go of her.

He learned to roll with whatever she handed him, and for a while it was okay, but he soon learned how miserable he was, and he could not keep living this way he was. This was before meeting Pablo Cruz.

Now, all he could think of was, *Well, she is resting in peace—no more pain, demons, or monkeys on her back.* He was still cleaning up the financial mess she'd made before her death. Lori became spiteful and malicious when Trey worked the long hours that were required in his practice One day she went into the operating room and threw a coffeepot at him that was full of coffee from the nurse's station. She screamed at him, "Are you ever going to come home?" She would hold everything against him and punish him by drinking. He could not speak to her when she was heavily intoxicated because she was extremely mean. She would sell off things that were special to him, like his motorcycle collection and his prized possessions. Lori could never forgive Trey for not giving her the attention she desired and longed for. She didn't enjoy being the trophy wife she had become. He'd thought he could never forgive her for the things she had done to him, but now he was learning just how little material things meant. Nothing could replace the void in his heart. He realized how much he truly loved her and how all the problems they had seemed so small compared to this.

CHAPTER 20

Two days had passed, and the office was shaping up to close. Patients were referred to other doctors and clinics for further treatment. Trey was sad but also relieved to be getting out of this town. He'd try to put his life back together.

"Okay, Dr. Martinez, the last of the hard copies of the patient files are boxed up and ready to be loaded."

"Thanks, Leti. Put them on the stack. All patient files have been loaded in the system so other doctors can access patients' information, right?"

"Yes, sir. It has been completed. There is another clinic on the phone wanting to ask about our ultrasound machines. Would you be interested in parting with any of them?"

"Sure," he responded. "The less I have to ship, the better. Tell them to come by as soon as he can today to meet with me, and we can work something out."

As the day progressed, the schedule dwindled down. Trey asked Leti about everybody's paychecks and severance pay. She replied, "I have the checks here."

"Okay. I want to go ahead and hand them out because I have a bonus for whoever stays late with me tonight to finish this up. It is going to be a long night, but I have a plane that will be waiting for me on the tarmac once I am finished."

"Okay, Dr. Martinez. I and three other staff members are going to stay."

"Great," he replied. "Order pizza and drinks for everyone, and let's get this done."

After all the patients were finished, Trey came out of the last exam room and told Leti how bittersweet it was to be giving everything up, because he had a great practice and an awesome staff. "I have never had the loyalty I've had with this crew, and I loved working with each and every one of you. Okay, enough of the sappy stuff. I am hungry. Is the pizza here? And what time is it?"

"The pizza and drinks are here, and it is now 11:00 p.m."

"Okay, how much more do we have before we can wrap this up?"

Leti said, "Well, we are just about to finish up. The rest will be up to the movers."

"Okay. I guess this is goodbye, then."

With tears in her eyes, she replied, "Yes, sir. I am going to miss you."

"I'm going to miss you too, Leti. I could not have gotten through all of this without you. Let me walk you to the door so I can lock myself in. Remember that you have to meet the movers in the morning to let them in. I added a small bonus for all the extra help. Thank you for everything. Until we meet again."

With tears running down her cheek, Leti went to the door. Dr. Martinez opened it for her. She hugged him and left. He then quickly locked it back up so no one could get in with him. The back doors had already been secured, so he knew he was the only one there. After he checked all the offices and rooms, he thought, *Well, it's time.*

He started to the door, and as he did so, a man approached him from the waiting area. "How did you get in here, and what can I do for you?"

The man blocked the doorway so Trey could not flee and laughed. "Dr. Martinez, you didn't think we forgot about you, did you?" As he said that, two men came from behind Trey. All he remembered was something hitting him in the head and everything going black.

CHAPTER 21

When Trey came to, he was sitting in a chair with his arms taped down to the arms of the chair, and his legs were taped to the legs of the chair. He could hardly move. He was gagged with a rag in his mouth, and blood trickled down his face from where he'd been hit in the head. He woke with a sharp pain to the back of his head, and it made his vision blurry.

"Welcome back, Doc. Glad to see you could make it." The voice was oh, so clear.

Wait a minute—I recognize that voice, he thought. Then when the thought popped into his mind, he knew exactly who it was: Pablo Cruz.

Pablo stood in front of him "I see you made it back to us, Dr. Martinez. Good, good. You are back, but let's see for how long." Pablo took out a pistol and began waving it around. "After what you did to my wife and child, you are lucky to be alive." As he finished the sentence, he swung the gun and hit Trey in the temple.

Trey's head flew to the side and dropped down. He was still conscious, and more blood poured out of his head. He told Pablo, "Just go ahead and kill me. Get it over with. You have taken everything that means anything to me as well. My wife did no harm to you, and you stabbed her like you were stabbing a pig. She was lucky to live as long as she did after that. She was an easy target."

"Shut up! I will cut out your tongue!" Pablo screamed. "You are not in charge now! I am, and you are going to die when I say you can." He motioned over for his guys to give Trey some smelling salts so Trey would be alert. "Now, do you see me clearly?"

Trey shook his head and said, "Yes, I do."

"Good. Let's get started. I want one of your fingers."

"What?" Trey responded.

"You heard me. Can you answer me, or do I choose for you? Oh, what the hell. Let's take all five on that hand."

They taped Trey's hand down so he could not move it at all. They took a pair of pliers out that were sharp and designed for this type of work. They placed the pliers under and on top of Trey's first finger and started to press, Trey screamed at the top of his lungs in pain. Finally, the finger snapped off, and blood rushed everywhere. Trey was panting, sweating, and breathing hard. Then the guy took a hot soldering iron that they had heated up, and he cauterized the finger to stop the bleeding. Trey screamed even louder. As they finished, the air smelled of burned flesh, and Trey vomited.

"Now, now, Doc, It wasn't that bad, was it?"

"I don't know, you son of a bitch. Why don't you sit in the chair and take a couple of yours off?"

"It's going to be a long night, and I want you to be here with me. Let's give him a small break and then start on the next one. Give him some smelling salts again so he is fully awake. I am bored, so I am going to sit in the front until you are finished."

The guys started, and all one could hear was the screaming getting louder and louder. Then there was the smell. When they finished with the one hand, Trey was unconscious and slumped over in the chair. All the bleeding had stopped, but the smell of burned flesh lingered in the air. It smelled like someone had died.

"Okay," Pablo yelled, "let's wake him up and see where we can start this time."

Just before getting him awake, someone knocked on the door. "Dr. Martinez, are you in there?" It was the security officer that Trey had hired to look after the office until the stuff had shipped out. "Hello? I hear you in there. Please open the door."

Pablo opened the door and told the guard that no one was in the office; they were there to finish up some packing for the doctor.

The guard looked around and felt something was wrong, but he said nothing because he saw the gun sticking out of the back of Pablo's jeans. "Okay, then. I'll let you guys get back to it. Sorry I bothered you."

Pablo closed and locked the door and went to the back where Trey was being held. "We are going to have to wrap this up. It looks like this guy had someone checking on his office."

As Pablo said that, he walked over to Dr. Martinez. Hook out a long hunting knife and stabbed the doctor. He raised the knife and said, "I want you to remember Mia." He did this three more times in the abdomen until the doctor went unconscious. "Let's give him a little juice."

As soon as he gave the order to the guys, they sat up Trey, gave him some smelling salts, and brought him somewhat around. Then they began to hook him up. Trey was attached to a machine that delivered electrical currents at different voltages. It was set on the lowest setting to begin with. They flipped it on to see if it worked, and Trey got stiff and shook his head in the chair.

The men looked at Pablo and said, "It's ready." Trey slumped forward again as soon as they cut off the machine. They turned the voltage up to a higher setting and started the machine again, this time for about thirty seconds. Then they cut it off again.

Pablo walked over to Trey. "Wow, it works. Looks like you pissed yourself."

Trey looked at Pablo and said, "You would too if your dick was hooked to that machine."

"Turn it up higher, and let's see how he and his dick takes this. Then we can finish it off."

Trey screamed again as his body shook and jerked around.

Pablo said, "Okay stop. Dr. Martinez, your time is up!"

CHAPTER 22

Just as dawn began to break, cop sirens blared and lights flashed on the cars that sped into the parking lot where Dr. Trey Martinez had his office. The security guard had called the police as soon as he saw Pablo Cruz was in the office. Officer Espinoza asked the guard to open the door. When he did, they realized the alarm was not set, so they knew someone had been in there. They called out, "Anyone in here? Please come out. Hello, anyone?"

As they came around the corner, the office smelled like something was burned, but it had a distinctive odor—it smelled like human flesh. "Search the front offices, and I'll do the back."

They found Dr. Martinez bound with no fingers and slumped over in a chair with voltage leads still hooked up to him. "I found him!" Espinoza called out. "Call for an ambulance and tell them to hurry. Help me get him off the chair and lay him flat. Let's see. Does he have a pulse?"

"Very faint. This poor bastard went through pure hell."

Trey's skin was black where the electrodes were placed, and his arms and legs were so stiff they could hardly move him. "I don't think I have ever seen it this bad before. On this hand, all his fingers are cut off."

"Yes, I see that."

"Pick up his fingers, and let's get some ice to preserve them—if he makes it. Maybe they can attach one or two, or even all five. Just preserve them! The ambulance is here move. Out of the way and let them work. Get him to the hospital ASAP. Every minute will count—if we aren't too late already. Let's roll."

As the ambulance drove off, Officer Espinoza looked around and saw someone move around the building. He went to check it out.

"Hello, Officer David Espinoza," a voice called out from around the corner. Pablo Cruz stood there, daring the officer to arrest him.

"What are you still doing here?"

"I came to give you your money. I could not have pulled this off without you. You giving me all the information about the doctor was crucial to my revenge."

Espinoza said, "You can't do this here. What if someone sees you?"

"No one is here. Take the bag—it's all there. Enjoy your payday. You earned it. That's more than you make in a year. Hell, that's more than you make in five years." Pablo laughed.

Officer Espinoza said, "Pablo, please don't come back to this area anytime soon. I have been on this police force for twenty-two years, and I can't keep cleaning up your messes. I don't think I can keep covering up bullshit like this. That doctor was a good man, and look what you did to him! It was cruel and disgusting! You need to get your ass back to Mexico before someone recognizes you."

"You know how I feel about family, David! Don't forget she was your *Cunada* and my son was your *sobrino.* You are lucky you are my brother, or I would have had you killed a long time ago for talking to me as harshly as you do."

"Go home, Pablo. I am sure your next wife is waiting."

Pablo laughed again, looked back at David, and said, "I'm sure she is. Bien por hermano."

CHAPTER 23

The ambulance arrived at the hospital, and a team of doctors was called in to work on Trey.

"Let's get him out and roll him into bay one. He looks like he has been through a meat grinder. His face is beat all to hell."

"Is he viable?"

"Barely. Let's see if we can get him hooked up to the monitors and get him to surgery."

Just then, Trey crashed. "Code blue to the emergency room!"

Everyone came running, and after thirty minutes one could see by the faces of the staff that it did not look good. After forty-five minutes, they were still working on Dr. Martinez.

"I am sorry, but he is still unresponsive. Let's call it. Time of death is 8:30 a.m."

"What a way to start the day on such a sad note. Call administration."

Mr. Dan Brown was the CEO of the hospital and wanted to be notified if any staff or doctors were admitted or worked on at the facility. Mr. Brown came straight to the emergency room and took a peek under the sheet. "Wow! He looks horrible! We are going to have to step up security around here." Mr. Brown approached the nurse's station and asked, "Does anyone know who the next of kin is for Dr. Martinez?"

No one answered. Dr. Martinez had started there only a couple of months ago. As Mr. Brown walked back to his office with his head hung low, he thought about having to call his son, who was in the Dallas area. *This is such a terrible thing for Dr. Martinez and his family. And let's not forget the hospital has lost money on him.* Mr. Brown was a numbers man, and he was always worried about the bottom dollar because he wanted to make sure the hospital was profitable.

When he walked into his office, he sat down at his desk and asked his assistant to bring Dr. Martinez's file into his office, as well as a cup of coffee. He started looking for Dr. Martinez's contact info, hoping his son's phone number or information was in there.

As he was reading through the paperwork, his assistant knocked at the door and said, "Excuse me, Mr. Brown. This just came for you."

He looked up and saw he had an arrangement of flowers and a box someone had sent to him. "Oh, I could use some good news today after the morning I have had with Dr. Martinez's passing." He opened the box and saw a beautiful red bow. "Aw, that's nice." He reached in and pulled out the item. Inside was a beautiful red bow wrapped around a gift. Then he saw it. "Oh my God!" It was a slab of human skin with a perfectly placed red bow. The freshly skinned human skin was folded like a shirt.

"What the hell is this?" He yelled for his assistant. "Is this some kind of a sick joke? Who sent this sick thing to me?"

His assistant ran into the office and said, "This lady just dropped it off for you and asked me to place it on your desk with the flowers. She told me you were going to be sad today, so I brought them in here for you. I thought they would cheer you up."

He reached down and opened the card on the flowers. It read, "Thank you for hiring the piece of shit Dr. Martinez who killed my wife and child. Here is a souvenir for you. I did to him what he did to my family. I hope you don't mind me showing my appreciation. Signed, Pablo Cruz."

Printed in the United States
By Bookmasters